I0728471

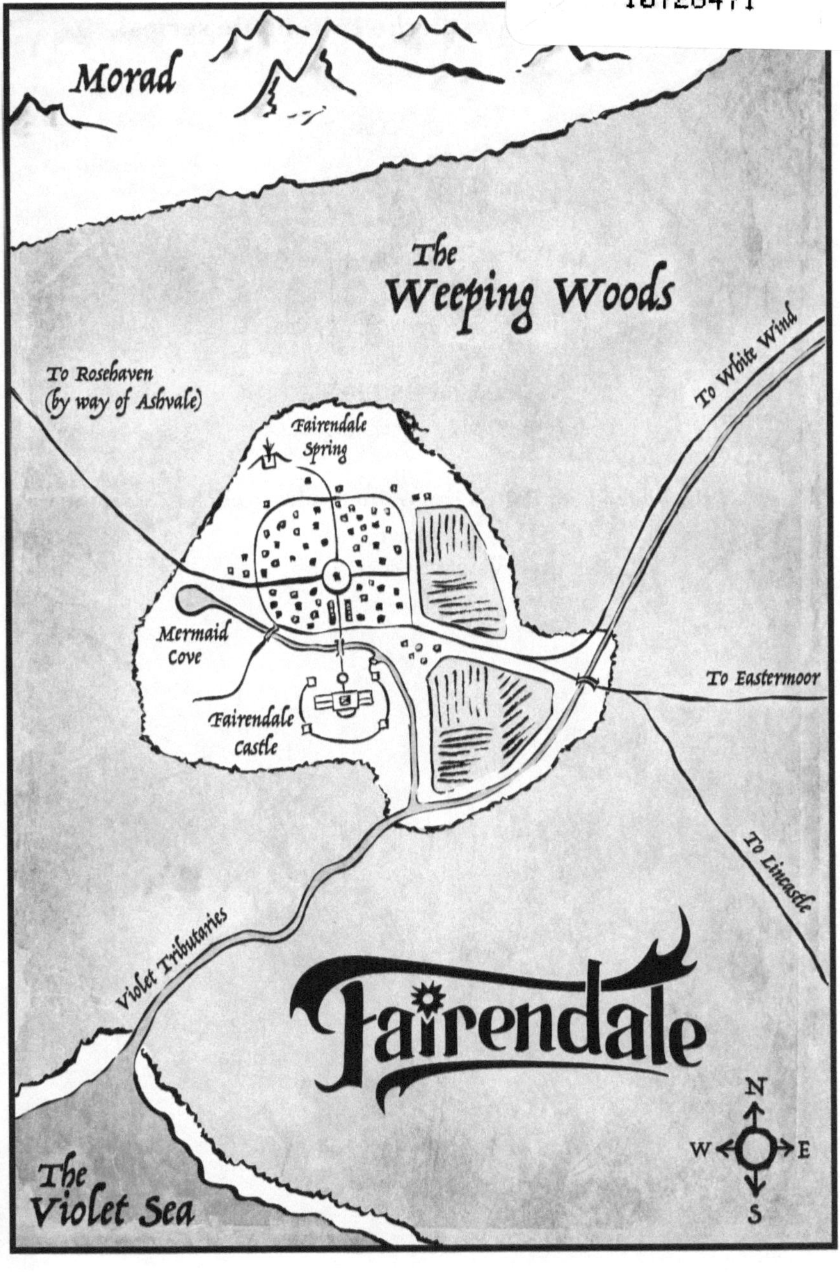

Morad
The Weeping Woods
To Rosehaven (by way of Ashvale)
To White Wind
Fairendale Spring
Mermaid Cove
Fairendale Castle
To Eastermoor
To Lincastle
Violet Tributaries
Fairendale
The Violet Sea
N
W
E
S

Read all the books in the Fairendale series!

Book .5: *The Good King's Fall (a prequel)*
Book 1: *The Treacherous Secret*
Book 2: *The King's Pursuit*
Book 3: *The Perilous Crossing*
Book 4: *The Dragons of Morad*
Book 5: *The Fiery Aftermath*
Book 6: *The Mysterious Separation*

Collector's Editions:
Books 1-6: *The Flight of the Magical Children*

To see all the books L.R. Patton has written, please click or visit the link below:
www.lrpatton.com/store

Fairendale

6

THE MYSTERIOUS SEPARATION

Batlee Press
PO Box 591596
San Antonio, TX 78259

L.R. PATTON

THE MYSTERIOUS SEPARATION

BATLEE
PRESS

To the invisible ones
You are seen
and known

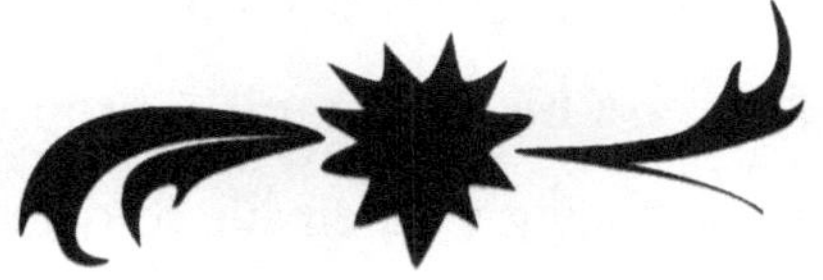

Sacrifice

Let us begin our journey today in the dungeons beneath the dungeons, inside the royal castle of Fairendale, the most beautiful of all kingdoms in our fairy tale land.

Here, in this infinite blackness, Aleen, a prophet of one hundred forty-two years, is not sleeping, though all the children and prophets behind her are. They have run out of light in this prison, you see, a prison where they have remained since King Willis ordered them here. The boy, Calvin, who has brought their provisions day after day, has not visited in some time, though Aleen cannot be sure quite how long it has been since he last left them. The children do not like lying awake in darkness, and so they sleep, until light can be found again.

Aleen is thinking. She has been thinking since the last candle burned out. She is thinking of what is coming.

You see, Aleen has learned from Yerin that she is very near

her one hundred forty-third birthday. A prophet's one hundred forty-third birthday is a very special one in the time of a prophet —the only birthday when they might summon one last spell of magic. And while that may seem like quite a generous gift from this magical land, it must be said that if a prophet decides to use that one bit of magic, they give their life to do so. A prophet will die for magic, if she so chooses.

This is what occupies the mind of our prophetess. Should she risk her own life for the sake of the children? Should she remain here and bear what is to come? Should she set something entirely different in motion?

Aleen reaches for Yerin's hand. He is the only prophet awake in the dungeons. Truth be told, he is the only prophet strong enough to wake. The others have fallen into a deep sleep, having been without sunlight and warmth and a full table of food for far too long. Yerin touches Aleen's shoulder.

"What is it you will do?" he says in the gentlest whisper he can manage.

"I do not know," Aleen says. "But the children."

"You will die," Yerin says, and if we could see through the dark, we would see a single tear pass across Yerin's white-stubbled cheek.

"Yes. I will die," Aleen says. "But I do not have much of life left."

"You would if we escaped from this dungeon," Yerin says.

"And you have Seen our escape?" Aleen says.

The two, you see, have talked long and quiet, as the children slept behind them. Aleen knows what it is that Yerin has Seen. It is not, alas, good news. But there is something Aleen can do. A circuitous route, to be sure, but something that might change the vision Yerin has shared.

"No," Yerin says.

Aleen pats his knee. "All will be well, Yerin," she says.

"But you will die," he says. His voice breaks, and he clears his throat.

"Hush, now," Aleen says, as though she is speaking to one of the children. "We must not wake the children."

They are quiet for a time. And then Yerin says, "You have never told me why it is you lost your Sight when you came to this dungeon."

"I do not understand it myself," Aleen says. "I suspect it is because my Sight is connected to the Old Man's Great Book."

"The Old Man's Great Book?" Yerin says. "How came you to possess such a treasure?"

"I studied beneath the Old Man," Aleen says. "He passed the book on to me when he died."

Yerin grows quiet once more. He is thinking of another woman, a young woman he knew many years ago, who studied beneath the Old Man. A young woman he loved and lost.

Their hands find one another in the dark, as if they always belonged entwined. And at the precise moment when fingers lock around fingers, a great vision plays across Yerin's mind.

Oh, yes. There will be a sacrifice. And it will be brilliant.

He squeezes Aleen's hand. She smiles in the dark, though no one can see her. They fall into a patchy sleep, together.

Not enough time has passed for Captain Sir Greyson to return to the kingdom of Fairendale. He was sent out to scour the other kingdoms for more men, after his died in the fiery dragon lands. But Sir Greyson, truth be told, has no heart left in him. He is returning to Fairendale a beaten man. He did not even make it to the first distant land before he turned on his heel and began walking home.

So he is walking, slowly, tiredly, back to the village, where he will kneel before his mother and tell her how he has failed her this time. He is an honorable man, of course, but this he simply cannot do. He cannot keep chasing children. He cannot continue to build an army that will serve only the king's best interest. He cannot do whatever the king bids any longer, and so he knows that his mother will most likely die by this decision, for a man who defies the king is a man who will not receive the medical provisions necessary to keep his mother alive. He would be the one to tell her himself.

Though the crueler of the kingdom's faithful people, were any to exist, might berate Sir Greyson for his cowardice—for a man who knows a mission is doomed before it even begins and so abandons that mission is a man ridiculed for his decision—we know that he has, perhaps, chosen the more honorable thing: defy a king and save the children.

It is true that the neighboring kingdoms do not look so kindly on Fairendale now that the news has traveled of what King Willis has done to the children. It is true that, even now, as we speak, another king is writing angry correspondence to King Willis, demanding that he let the imprisoned children go free. (You might be wondering who this other king could possibly be. But you must be patient, dear reader. That is a story for another time.) It is true that King Willis will hear advice from no one, until the missing children are found and his throne is secured for good.

Sir Greyson nears the edge of Fairendale's land, and the cold ball of fear moves from his chest to his throat. He does not want to return to the castle at all, for he does not want to face the wrath of King Willis. Sir Greyson knows nothing of what has passed in his absence. He does not realize that Prince Virgil has been taken by the village people and stowed away somewhere, safe from watching eyes.

He moves through the village's quiet streets, his feet aching beneath him. And though he would like nothing more than to stop at his mother's house, he does not. He simply continues on his way, his head drooping, his steps shuffling, his pace somewhat slower than it had been moments before. He must return to the castle. He must be honest with the king. He must finish the job, though the king will surely relieve him of his duties once he discovers what Sir Greyson has not done.

He misses his mother. Does she yet live? He will know soon enough. But it will not be soon enough for him.

Sir Greyson knocks on the door of the castle. It is quiet and still. He knocks again. Surely someone is still here. Surely they have not all abandoned this great structure of stone and iron. Surely the dragons have not attacked while he walked the lands aimlessly. Sir Greyson feels a pinch in his chest. He opens the castle doors, unsure of what he will find. The hallways are as quiet as the exterior. His steps echo on the marble floors. He heads straight for the throne room.

There is no one stationed at the double doors, so Sir Greyson pulls them open, with great effort, himself. The king is hunched over his throne, his head in his hands. He looks as if he has deflated a bit. Has the king stopped eating? Has his stomach shrunk in the days since Sir Greyson has been gone?

Sir Greyson does not know where to begin. He clears his throat. King Willis looks up.

"Captain," he says, and he straightens a little in his seat.

"Sire," Sir Greyson says. He draws nearer, unable to speak another word. It is the exhaustion, perhaps, or the sadness, or the failure. He does not quite know what stays his tongue.

But he has no need to say anything at all, for King Willis says, "My son," in the exact place where Sir Greyson had expected him to say "What news do you have for me?" Sir Greyson stops on his way up the red carpet.

"Your son, sire?" he says. "Has something happened while I have traveled?" He clears his throat again, as if to cover up the lie, though it is not really a lie so much as it is an exaggeration. Sir Greyson did not travel. He merely wandered.

King Willis rises from the throne. His eyes are tortured, red, as though he has been crying. Sir Greyson has never seen his king cry. Might the prince be dead?

"Is the prince well?" Sir Greyson says.

"They have taken him," King Willis says, and Sir Greyson is more confused than ever.

"Who has taken him?" he says. The dragons? What would the dragons want with a boy?

"The people," King Willis says, and he flings an angry hand

behind him, back toward the village of Fairendale. "The people have taken my son."

Sir Greyson sucks in a breath. The village people? They have taken the prince? His mind whirls with the possibilities. Perhaps the king will let the children go. Perhaps he will call off the search. Perhaps the village will return to its former beauty.

And then Sir Greyson asks the next question that baffles him. "How?" he says.

"While you were gone," the king says, and now his eyes turn angry, as if it were Sir Greyson's fault he was not at the castle to protect it from the villagers.

Sir Greyson does not want to draw his king's attention to why he was gone in the first place, so he says, "Who took your son?"

"The village people," the king shouts, though Sir Greyson already knows this.

"Who among the village people?" Sir Greyson says.

King Willis waves his hand. His eyes crackle black. "A woman with flames for hair and eyes the color of the castle lawn." King Willis pauses for a moment, blinks, breathes, and then, "As it used to be."

There is only one woman in the village with flames for hair and eyes the color of the castle lawn. Cora.

Sir Greyson's heart clenches. What has she done?

"I have sent everyone away," King Willis says, "to search." The king's shoulders slump once more. "There is no bread. There are no cakes. There is no Cook."

Of course Cook would be the one person King Willis would miss the most. Is this where his sadness lies? Does he feel sorrier for the loss of Cook or the loss of his son?

"Queen Clarion," Sir Greyson says. "She is safe?"

King Willis waves his hand. "Yes, of course," King Willis says. "What would the people want of her?"

"And everyone else has gone searching for your son?" Sir Greyson says, still trying to understand.

"Searching for my son?" King Willis says. "No, they have not gone searching for my son. They have gone to find the missing children."

Sir Greyson stares at his king. What must it be like to care more for finding a magic boy than finding your missing son? He cannot imagine it.

"The servants are gone?" Sir Greyson says. "Cook?"

"She disappeared into the woods and did not return," King Willis says.

"Garth?" Sir Greyson says.

The king tilts his head. His eyes narrow. "Garth? Who is this Garth? I do not know anyone named Garth."

Sir Greyson thinks it better not to mention that Garth is the boy who does whatever the king bids. But perhaps he should have, for the next moment King Willis says, "Where are your men?" as if noticing for the first time that Sir Greyson has entered the throne room alone.

The captain clears his throat. He does not say what is jumbled in his mind to say—that the people in other kingdoms would not come to the aid of Fairendale if he were to travel and ask them this favor; that a man he met on his way, early on, told him people all across the lands have begun calling King Willis a tyrant, like his father before him; that he did not, in fact, do what he was bid to do.

Instead, he says, "Perhaps it is time to let the children go, sire."

It is quite astonishing how quickly the eyes of King Willis can move from the softest brown to the darkest black. Their flash causes Sir Greyson to take a single step back. "Never," King Willis says. "I will never let them go now."

"Perhaps they will trade your son for their children," Sir Greyson says.

"Never," King Willis says. "I will never give in to the demands of the people." He clenches his teeth together. "They will never win."

Sir Greyson knows the people of the village. He knows that winning has nothing to do with what they have done. But for a man like King Willis, the possibility is impossible to imagine. So Sir Greyson merely keeps it to himself.

"Have they made demands?" Sir Greyson says.

"Of course they have," King Willis says. His arm sweeps the throne room. "They are not foolish people, I will give them that much."

"You are vulnerable here, without men to protect you," Sir Greyson says.

King Willis turns on his captain with a rage that is terrifying. Sir Greyson is glad that he is ten paces away and that King Willis would have to walk down four steps to reach him. He has never seen his king walk down steps without the aid of his page. "That is what you were supposed to bring me," King Willis says.

From somewhere deep within him, Sir Greyson finds the courage to tell his king the truth. "Our neighbors will not come," he says. "They do not believe in your ways."

King Willis lets loose the loudest growl Sir Greyson has ever heard. The king's face turns red and then purple before he is finished. His hands ball into fists, and he raises them toward Sir Greyson. "You will find me men," he says. "Or you shall be dismissed."

"There are no men to be found, sire," Sir Greyson says. "I am prepared for your dismissal."

The two men stare at one another for a time. King Willis

grows calmer. Sir Greyson grows braver. "They only want their children, sire," he says.

"They will not have their children," King Willis says. "They can have my food and my provisions and the ornate beauty of this castle, but they will never have their children."

It is clear to Sir Greyson, dear reader, that King Willis has crossed beyond mere pursuit and into dangerous obsession, for it is obsession that can twist a heart so wildly that one cannot see reason or strategy or even truth beyond what one believes is truth. King Willis, you see, believes that the unarguable truth is he must capture all the children or he will face a death so brutal it cannot be told in stories.

And though it seems quite ridiculous to us that a king might die if he does not secure a throne, for man can surely live a full and happy life without ruling a kingdom, there is a reason our king believes this, of course, as there is reason that every man and woman and child believe what they believe. But we are getting ahead of ourselves.

Sir Greyson is not finished with King Willis. "Perhaps you might return the children who do not have magic. Perhaps we can send them back to their parents and they will be satisfied with a compromise. Perhaps then they will release your son."

King Willis shakes his head, a vigorous one that makes his curly hair, wisps the color of sand, flap about his face. "No," he says. He points at Sir Greyson. "You will find my son. We will keep the children."

Sir Greyson sighs. He hoped this would be over. He hoped he might return to his mother and nurse her for her final days, for once he leaves the service of the king, she will not have access to the medicine that keeps her living. The captain dips his head. "As you wish, sire," he says.

"Find my son," King Willis says. "Bring him back. And if they will not willingly give him, you shall take him." The last words are spoken as one might speak a whispery threat, intended to bring fear to whomever hears it. Whispered words, with the right force and face behind them, are much more terrifying than the loudest ones. King Willis has perfected this art, for he watched well his father before him.

Watches him still.

But wait. I am afraid I have shared something this story is not quite ready to share. Yes, well, forget I said a word.

For now, let us turn our attention back to our captain and the king. Sir Greyson has just shivered, the whispered words of King Willis walking down his spine and back up his chest. "Very well, sire," Sir Greyson says. "Right away."

He spins on his heel and moves toward the door. But before he has left the king's presence entirely, before the door has closed on his passing, he turns back. And what he sees takes the shiver that crosses his back and chest and turns it into an ice-cold sword that burns through his belly.

The king, you see, has lifted the curtain on whatever it is that has sat next to his throne since he inherited the kingship. A mirror. Long and clear and golden at the oval edges. And though Sir Greyson cannot see the reflection in the mirror, he hears his king begin to speak.

King Willis, speaking to a mirror.

Whatever could it mean?

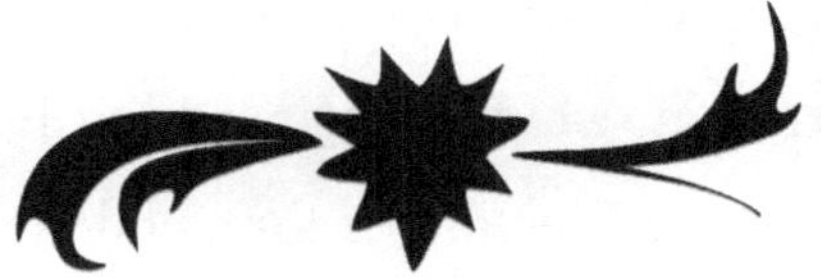

Escape

In the kingdom of White Wind, a girl was born many years ago. One hundred forty-two years, to be exact. This girl wore skin and hair as dark as the night on which she was born, and her mother and father gave her a royal name: Aleen.

She lost her mother early, when she was a girl of seven, and came to know only a life with her father. She thought of her mother often in those days, for the death had happened unexpectedly. Her mother collapsed in the streets one day, and Aleen watched her father drag her mother to bed. The town healer called it a fever, one that could not be cured. Death visited her mother two days later, though no one could see him. Aleen could only feel him.

Aleen blamed her father. He was not a kind man, you see. In fact, he rarely even let his wife or daughter outside the house, for he did not like it when they spoke to the other villagers. Aleen had no friends, no laughter, no excitement at all.

She was a wanderer at heart. She despised being locked in a house so full of her father's sweat smell. She longed to be free. She longed to walk the streets on her own, without his heavy hand holding her arm, whipping her behind him any time they passed another villager. She longed for a child of her own.

And soon she met a boy, on one of her late night wanderings. When her cottage rumbled with the sound of her father's breathing, Aleen would wander. It did not take her long to find Jeremy. It did not take her long to begin calling him Jem. It did not take her long to fall in love.

She loved him, and he loved her, but Aleen knew that her father would never allow her to marry. Jem had asked to speak with her father many times, of course, but Aleen told him not to bother. She knew he would never release her from her prison. He needed someone to keep house and prepare his meals and care for the sheep out behind their cottage.

"How do you know he will not set you free?" Jem said one night, when they sat beneath the moon, inside the woods, so anyone watching would not see them.

She had never told anyone why. But she knew she could trust Jem. She had known him for many days now. "I have a gift," she said.

"A gift?" he said. He tilted his head at her.

"A gift for reading the hearts and intentions of people," she said. "I know what is in their hearts. I know what they intend to do." She let the last words trail off in a whisper.

"Sounds a bit like magic," Jem said.

"Yes, well," Aleen said. "It is why my father has hidden me all these years. He is afraid of what the people will say."

"We must get you away from him," Jem said.

"I wish for it every day," Aleen said.

"Then run away with me," he said. "Run away with me and never come back."

"You know I cannot do this," Aleen said.

"We could become different people," he said. "He would never find us."

Aleen looked at him then, her eyes searching his face. Whatever could he mean, become different people?

"You have the gift of magic," Jem said.

"No," Aleen said. "It is simply a way of seeing."

"It is magic," Jem said. "Your father has not told you the truth."

"Magic?" Aleen said. "But why would not my mother—"

"Perhaps your mother did not know," Jem said.

Aleen thought of it for a time. Her mother had never said a word about magic, but Aleen had only been a young girl when her mother died. There were other things on her mind then.

Perhaps her mother had been waiting for the right time.

"And I…" Jem grew very quiet. Aleen looked at him. His eyes flashed in the moonlight. "I have magic as well."

Aleen drew back from him, as if he were something dangerous. And, in the kingdom of White Wind, boys with magic were considered very dangerous, for stories told of men who had stolen everything that was valuable, including a highly prized magic sword from within the kingdom's walls, simply because they had magic. Magic was looked upon with disgust and mistrust by the people who had to begin anew all over again every time magic crossed its borders.

"Do not be afraid," Jem said. "I have lived here all my life. With magic."

Aleen did not know what to say.

"I did not tell you because I did not know if I could trust you completely," Jem said. "But I knew, this day, when you told me your secret, that I could trust you with mine." Jem leaned closer. "You are not afraid of me, are you?" He peered into her eyes, and they were the same eyes they had always been.

Nothing had changed about him at all. Just her knowledge of him.

"No," she said.

They were quiet for a time.

"With magic, we could transform ourselves," Jem said. "We

would not look the same, and your father would never know. To him, we would simply vanish."

Aleen looked at this boy she loved, and she felt the tug of her heart. "Is it not dangerous?" she said. The stories in her kingdom also spoke dark and dangerous words about magic. Some of it was true. Some of it was not in the least.

"Perhaps a bit," Jem said. "A transformation spell is not nearly so dangerous as a vanishing spell. But it carries its own risks."

"What sorts of risks?" Aleen said.

Jem smiled at her with half of his mouth. "You could become a girl of twenty-two. I could become a boy of thirteen."

Aleen laughed. She could not help it.

"But that is only with unpracticed magic," Jem said. "A sorcerer controls a transformation spell."

"But my magic would only be unpracticed," Aleen said. "I have never done magic."

"You have done magic," Jem said. "You were simply not aware of it." He took her hand. "But I shall teach you."

She smiled at him.

"And what would we do after we transform ourselves?" Aleen said.

"We would run away," Jem said. "To another land."

"How would we get there?" Aleen said.

"By foot," Jem said.

"By foot?" Aleen said. "The closest land to us is Guardia." She shivered. "Not a place I would want to be."

"There are other lands," Jem said. "We would reach them before anyone would track us."

"What makes you so sure of that?" Aleen said.

Jem shrugged. "Or we could use a vanishing spell." His eyes grew dark, serious. He looked at her. "I know how to do those as well."

"Where is it you learned your magic?" Aleen said.

"From an old prophet outside the borders of White Wind," Jem said. "I found him on one of my hunts."

They lapsed into a silence that felt quite comfortable, both of them thinking of what this escape might mean for their future. Jem knew very well the risks of a vanishing spell. Aleen had no idea. But she knew very well the risks of leaving her father.

A blackbird called over their heads. They both looked up, and perhaps it was the bird, or perhaps it was the gentle moon, that made Aleen say, "Very well."

"Very well?" Jem said. His eyes held questions.

"We shall run away," Aleen said.

Jem smiled and wrapped his arms around her. Aleen fell against him softly. "First I shall have to teach you magic."

She laughed into his shoulder, but it did not even contain a fraction of the joy she felt.

Trust

Hazel sits alone at the table of the Enchantress, staring out the window in the direction where she knows her mother and the other children crowd into a house shaped like a shoe, though she cannot see it. How she misses them. The Enchantress ignores her mostly, going about her business, studying her books, tending to flowers. Watching her reminds Hazel of Mercy, who always loved to tend flowers. She was always helping Garron, the village gardener, tend the most colorful parts of Fairendale, while he saw to the parts that would feed and nourish the people. She does not know why the Enchantess keeps her here, away from the children and her mother.

Today, the Enchantress stands at the window, staring in the same direction Hazel is looking. Her voice is startling when she speaks. "Do you miss them?" A note of longing turns Hazel's eyes toward the beautiful, mysterious woman.

"Yes," Hazel says. "More than anything."

The Enchantress turns toward Hazel. She is dressed in a rich green gown that puffs out around the waist and all the way to her feet. The neck is high and trimmed with gold. Hazel has not seen her wear the same dress yet, though she has not lived here for so very long. She tears her eyes from the woman and glances about the house. It is old and musty, as if it has been here for a very long time.

"Would you like to see them?" the Enchantress says.

"Yes," Hazel says, her gaze returning to the milky white face. "Very much."

"Perhaps we shall arrange it," the Enchantress says. She looks away. "When it is safer."

"Yes," Hazel says, for she knows not what else to say. "When it is safer."

"Would you like a bit of bread?" The Enchantress says. She is already reaching for a plate, for Hazel has taken every offering the Enchantress has held out to her.

"That would be wonderful," Hazel says. Her voice is soft and sad, though the light in her eyes has not dimmed completely, for Hazel is a child who hopes even in the most dire of circumstances. She hopes that she will be reunited with her mother, Maude, and her father, Arthur, and her twin brother Theo. She hopes that the Enchantress will tell her soon why it is she is here. She hopes that they might one day, sooner rather than later, return to their home, for she never wanted to leave Fairendale in the first place.

The Enchantress slips the plate in front of her, and Hazel eats slowly, as if her stomach does not long for the bread. "Your magic," the Enchantress says. "Has it grown stronger since you have been here?"

Hazel swallows a bite and considers this question for a moment. Her magic has not grown stronger, but it has also not grown weaker. That means Theo must still be alive, somewhere. "Perhaps," she says. "I do not have much opportunity to practice it."

"Perhaps we should provide some opportunities," the Enchantress says. Hazel drops the bread. It clicks against her plate. The Enchantress tilts her head. "What is it?"

Hazel shakes her head. "Nothing," she says, for she cannot tell this woman, who is unknown, and, perhaps, untrustworthy, why it is that she cannot practice magic but must conserve what little power still remains. Every bit of magic one twin does outside of the presence of the other twin weakens their power considerably. Until Theo is back with Hazel, she must not perform any magic.

"Would you like an opportunity?" the Enchantress says. She watches Hazel closely.

"Perhaps," Hazel says.

"Your powers must not grow weaker," the Enchantress says. She hands Hazel another slice of bread. "You must not forget."

"I could not forget what I have learned," Hazel says.

"What your father taught you?" the Enchantress says.

"Yes," Hazel says.

"Tell me, how is it that he knew magic so well?" the Enchantress says.

"My mother had the gift," Hazel says. "He always wanted to learn."

"And you are sure he had none?" the Enchantress says.

No. Hazel has never been sure her father did not have the gift of magic. It is true that Maude and Arthur told her that her father did not have a bit of magic in his bones, but how is it that they could have produced two magical children? Was it not only the most powerful magic, combined together, that could produce twins? She had never entirely believed her mother and father, truth be told.

"I see that you have wondered as well," the Enchantress says.

"They would not tell stories," Hazel says. "Not to Theo and —" She realizes her error nearly as soon as the words are out.

The Enchantress does not blink but merely smiles. "Your brother," she says. "Of course I knew of your brother. It is why I asked." The Enchantress leans closer. "Twins do not come to just anyone."

Hazel notices, for perhaps the first time, that the woman's eyes are kind and soft. They are familiar eyes, yet she cannot place them. The Enchantress reaches across the table and touches Hazel's hand. Her skin is smooth and lovely. "You can trust me, Hazel," she says, and for a moment, Hazel is shaken by the voice, as if memory lives in it, waiting to be unlocked. But the moment is gone, and the Enchantress rises from her place. She returns to the window.

"Your mother is very brave," she says.

"Yes," Hazel says. "She is braver than she knows."

"And your father?" the Enchantress says. Is it her imagination, or does Hazel hear a catch in the woman's throat? "He lives?"

Hazel's eyes fill now. "We do not know," she says, as evenly as she can manage. Her father disappeared in the dragon lands. He might very well be among the men whose bodies were strewn about the desert for all of an afternoon and an evening before disappearing completely.

"It is as I feared," the Enchantress says, so softly that perhaps Hazel was not meant to hear the words, for they are puzzling words from a woman she has never known.

They lapse into a comfortable silence, one in which Hazel

considers all the people she has lost. Theo. Arthur. Mercy.

Oh, Mercy. Her best friend. It was Mercy who saved them from the underground portal, when a soldier found a shoe and broke the only link they had to the outside world. Mercy performed the most daring of spells: vanishing. The rules of magic are complicated. Mercy might return, but she would look nothing like she'd looked before—older or younger or lovelier or homelier or taller or shorter or less human-like and more animal-like. Or she might return and look every bit like she did before.

Or she might never return.

One could never know when magic took control, as it did so willingly in a vanishing spell. It was said that magic kept its hold over a sorcerer so that no one would vanish lightly. Magic demands a price, you see.

"Where did you lose sight of your father?" the Enchantress says when the silence has stretched between them for too long.

"In the dragon lands," Hazel says. "Many died there."

"And you believe he did as well?" the Enchantress says.

"No," Hazel says, but the word comes out in a rush of tears. "No," she says again, before burying her face in her hands. Somewhere in the middle of her weeping a hand touches her shoulder and then wraps all the way around her. The Enchantress holds her tight.

Hazel did not expect such warmth. She lifts her face, caught by the eyes of the woman before her. "All will be well," the Enchantress says. "You shall see."

Hazel nods, for she cannot speak.

The Enchantress rises again. Hazel stares at the wet spot on her sleeve. Does it belong to Hazel's tears or to those of the Enchantress?

"When might I see my mother?" Hazel says.

"Soon," the Enchantress says. "You shall see her soon. And the other children as well."

"Are they well?" Hazel says.

The Enchantress smiles. Her red lips stretch across straight white teeth. "Of course," she says. "They have more than they could ever need."

"Thank you," Hazel says, for this is enough for today. She does not ask what the Enchantress wants of her. She does not know the woman well enough yet. She will save that question for later. For now, Hazel returns the plate to a washing basin and gazes out the window.

"You miss your brother," the Enchantress says.

"Yes," Hazel says. "We have never been separated from one another."

"Perhaps we shall see him again someday," the Enchantress says. "Your father and your brother."

"Do you think so?" Hazel says. She dares not look at the Enchantress.

"Yes," the Enchantress says. "Yes, I believe we will."

Hazel turns toward the Enchantress, emboldened by her words. "And you will help me?" she says.

The Enchantress studies her for a moment. Hazel is terrified that she has said precisely the wrong thing at precisely the wrong time, but what was she to do with the kindness the Enchantress has shown today?

But then the woman's red lips pull once more into a smile, making her face beautifully young, and she says, "Of course." She floats away from the window, so very graceful she does not make a single bounce, and then she turns back to Hazel. "But you must stay here. You must not leave the house. There are dangers in these woods." She looks at Hazel one last time, and then she floats all the way out of the room. Hazel watches her go and then turns back to the window, where she studies the torched trees that surround this invisible house in the woods and the green ones that remain behind a concealment spell more powerful than any she could ever conjure. Her eye is caught by the flowers, by the promise of a shoe-shaped house on the other side of the clearing. She knows the Enchantress is correct in urging her to stay within the walls of the house, but she longs for her freedom nonetheless. If only there were a way to be free and safe at the same time.

She is startled by the Enchantress, returning to the room. The Enchantress carries a glowing ball and sets it on the table.

"What is this?" Hazel says, drawing nearer.

"A looking ball," the Enchantress says.

"I have never seen one," Hazel says. "Where did you get it?"

The Enchantress lifts a shoulder. "It was here in the house when I discovered it."

"So you have not always lived here?" Hazel says.

"Of course not," the Enchantress says. "I have only just come."

Hazel longs to ask more, such as why the Enchantress has come now and what it is she plans to do and who might have lived here before, but the Enchantress speaks again before she can summon the courage. "Your brother," the Enchantress says. "I cannot see him."

An ache begins in Hazel's chest and moves out toward her fingers. "He is dead?"

The Enchantress shakes her head. "No," she says. "We do not know for sure. Just because I cannot see him does not mean he does not live." She looks at Hazel and smiles, but it is not the same smile that she has turned on Hazel before. "It means that he is very good at hiding."

Hazel tries to steady her voice. "And my father?"

The Enchantress peers into the ball for some time. "He must be very good at hiding as well." She lifts the ball from the table. "I shall have to summon more powerful magic. But I am weary now." She takes the crystal ball and disappears into her room for quite some time.

Hazel is left alone at the table, to wonder at too many disturbing possibilities.

Though Sir Greyson has been charged with orders to find the missing prince, the first thing he does, instead, is visit his mother. He justifies this deviation from the king's orders by reasoning that the village people have stolen the boy, and perhaps his mother knows something about it. He shall at least try, and, in the meantime, assure himself that his mother still lives.

Fear touches the whole of his backside as he walks closer and closer toward the village. It is as silent and still as the castle was when he first walked in. He hopes the people have not all deserted this land. What would a land be without its people? The sky, on his walk, has grown darker, if that is even possible in this already-dark day. It looks as though it might rain, and not the kind of rain that sprinkles thirsty ground and lifts the faces of wilting flowers. The kind that will beat and thrash and bruise those caught in its wake. He stares at the dying flowers and passes a garden that looks as if it tries hard to hold on but does not have much hope. He hopes that this dying land does not foreshadow its people, but it is with a sense of deep foreboding that he opens the door of his mother's home.

She is not here. He searches every room, in and out and back again. His mother is not here. The room smells of sickness and medicine, and when he walks to the cabinets and opens them, not a single vial of healing tincture remains. He should not have left. He should never have left. Oh, what has he done?

Sir Greyson passes through the streets. He knocks on every door he passes. They all swing open, as if someone stands behind them, but there is no one here. At the door of the woman, Cora, he finds a note. It is written in code, as she used to write him when they were young.

Come to the fountain, it says.

Come to the fountain. Yes, he will come to the fountain.

It has been quite a long time since Sir Greyson has passed between the earth's layers and entered the secret room beneath the village fountains. He does not even remember when he last entered. Will he remember how to fall? Will he be denied entrance? He closes his eyes and tilts his body forward so it is falling. But his hands do not hit the ground. They pass through.

He stumbles into the lamplit room, and every eye is on him.

And Sir Greyson is so very glad to see the people of this village alive and well that he nearly begins to cry in front of every one of them. But instead he turns away.

A hand touches his shoulder. Sir Greyson turns to see the piercing green eyes of the woman he loved so long ago. "Cora," he says.

"Sir Greyson," she says. "You cannot be here." She looks behind her at the people who have begun to rise from their chairs, staring at him with twisted mouths and furrowed eyebrows and scowls that say he is anything but welcome here. "They all know you belong to the king."

"I do not belong to the king," Sir Greyson says, loud enough for all of them to hear. "I never belonged to the king." He turns back to Cora. "Never."

"But you became a king's man," Cora says.

"As my father did before me," Sir Greyson says. "No more and no less."

"The king tells you what to do," Cora says. "And you do it."

"No longer," Sir Greyson says. His eyes search hers. *I am on your side,* his say.

"But you took our children," Cora says. Her eyes narrow, full of so much hurt and anger and sadness that he cannot bear to see it. But he makes himself bear it, for it was his decisions that made these eyes.

"I did not take your children," Sir Greyson says. "I never wanted to take your children. The king…" He lets the words trail off, unsure that they will trust him, no matter what he says. "I only came to find my mother."

Cora tilts her head. Sir Greyson blinks. And then she nods, just once, and looks back at the people. "He only wants to see his mother," Cora says. "We should permit him."

"You are blind, Cora," a man says in a corner of the room. Sir Greyson almost does not recognize him. Bertie, the town's baker. "He belongs to the king, no matter what he says."

"No," Sir Greyson says. "I have left the king's service." It is untrue, as you will remember, but it is every bit of true in Sir Greyson's heart. For when a man makes a decision to do something, it becomes true in his mind. And Sir Greyson has already decided to leave the king. In fact, he did not come here to retrieve the prince at all. He came here to retrieve his mother, so the two of them might escape this cursed land.

"He stole our children," another woman says. Her blue eyes flash. Harsh. Angry. Dangerous. "We should kill him."

Cora holds up her hand. "My good people," she says. "He has only come to see his mother."

Sir Greyson hangs his head. The people grow quiet. Someone shuffles forward, and Sir Greyson dares look back up.

Garron stands before him. "My mother?" Sir Greyson says.

"First," Garron says. "You say you have left the king's service?"

"Yes," Sir Greyson says. "She will get no more medicine."

The people murmur around him. Perhaps they have come to understand what might drive a man like Sir Greyson, one of their own, to turn against them, if only for a moment in time.

Cora places her hand on Sir Greyson's arm. "She will die without her medicine," she says.

"Yes," Sir Greyson says. "I feared she was already dead." He looks about the room, but it is dark here. "I could not do what the king asked me to do. I came here to say my goodbyes." He came here, in truth, to take his mother with him, if she is strong enough.

Cora's face softens. "She is well," she says. "We raided the castle, and someone brought back some medicine. I have been tending her."

It is hard to contain true joy, true relief, and so it is that Sir Greyson's face, while breaking into a smile that is perhaps larger than what this dire situation might permit, also crumples into a grimace that ends in sobs so overwhelming that the man can only shake. The people turn away, preserving his dignity. Cora leads him toward his mother. She lies on a small cot set up in a cloaked corner of the room. She is smaller than he remembers.

He hardly recognizes her. Sir Greyson kneels before her. He feels the eyes of every person in this room watching him, but he does not care. He kisses his mother's wrinkled hand. "Mother," he says.

Her eyes flutter open. She looks painfully tired, as if she has been working vigorously all day, though Sir Greyson knows that it is vigorous enough work to draw the next breath. "My son," she says, her voice scratchy and weak. She reaches out a hand to pat his cheek. "I did not know if I would see you again." She smiles, her cracked lips stretching tight. "Now I may die in peace."

"No, Mother," Sir Greyson says. "Please. Stay. I have only just gotten here."

"I am old, son," she says. "I am tired."

"I know," Sir Greyson says, and he feels all the grief of the last days and weeks climbing on his back, all the disappointments and the poor decisions and the pointless chases that kept him from his mother's side. He can hardly lift his head beneath the weight of all those days he did not care for her. It pulls water from the deepest places in him. He shakes out cries and sobs and coughs as if he did not do this already. He tries to speak, but his mother cannot understand a single word.

"Hush, my dear," she says. She strokes his hair, as she did when he was a boy. "All will be well. You will see."

"I am sorry," he says, but she does not hear.

"I am proud of you," she says.

Sir Greyson pulls away then and looks at her with eyes that can hardly see her spotted skin. "I have done nothing," he says. He is drowning in this sea of grief, in this water that is too deep and too strong and too demanding. He grips her hand. She is his mother, you see, and she is dying, and he will never see her again, and he wasted so much time on all the things that did not matter. What if he had been here? What if he had spent his days not chasing after children but enjoying his mother's presence while he could?

It is strange what grief can do to a man. Some take it well, some rage, some cry, some close up tight, some ask questions. Sir Greyson is a man who asks questions. And the question that will not quiet is *What if?*

"You have done so much, my son," his mother says. "You have done so very much to help the kingdom." She breathes for a moment, as though she has forgotten how, and then she continues. "Now you must do something for yourself." She pats his cheek again. Her eyes stare into his, and he understands completely what it is they ask of him.

"Yes," he says. "I must do something for myself."

She closes her eyes, and he fears she has just died in his arms, but do not worry, dear reader. She is merely sleeping. She will not, in fact, die for many more months. It is only that she can feel the end coming, and she wants to make sure she tells her son what it is she needs to say before words leave her completely.

Sir Greyson turns to the men who continue to watch him, some with tears in their own eyes. There are few things harder in life than losing a parent. They all know it, too. Death and sickness, in a quite tragic and ironic way, bring men together.

"I know where the children are," Sir Greyson says.

A few of the people gasp. Cora takes a step forward. "Where are the children?" she says.

"In the dungeons beneath the dungeons," Sir Greyson says.

"The dungeons beneath the dungeons?" Garron says. "Who has heard of such a thing?"

"No one," Sir Greyson says. "That is why they have not been found."

"All the children?" Cora says.

"No," Sir Greyson says. "There are many missing. But perhaps we might at least reach the ones who can be reached."

"And you know how to get there?" Cora says.

"Yes," Sir Greyson says.

"You have a key?" Bertie calls out.

"No," Sir Greyson says. "But that will not be so hard to find."

Oh, dear reader. If only he knew.

"We must make a plan," Cora says.

"I will help," Sir Greyson says. "You need me."

Cora lets the people speak for her. "Lead us to the children," they say.

"First a plan," Sir Greyson says. "We must tread carefully."

"We need more food and supplies," Cora says.

"I can bring them to you," Sir Greyson says. "The castle is unguarded. There is no one to protect the king anymore."

The people murmur around him. Cora holds up her hand, and the people grow quiet. Sir Greyson stares at this woman who can command an entire village. She is more beautiful than he ever remembered her. "Then we shall move," she says.

"Yes," Sir Greyson says. "We shall move." Someone hands him a piece of parchment, and he bends before it, scratching out the map of the castle in ink.

Cora watches him, and as she watches, her face breaks into a smile.

Save

Jem taught Aleen all he knew of magic. First he made her a proper staff and showed her how to carry it and how to touch it and how to enchant it with the power of endless transformation so that it would not attract the notice of the village people. Her staff turned into a basket. His turned into a hat made of wood that one would only notice if one were close enough to admire the unique fibers.

Then Jem moved on to the magic instruction. Aleen learned quickly, and when he had reached the end of his knowledge, he said, "Now. It is time to make our plans."

And they did.

But it was not so easy as they had thought.

The night she was intended to meet Jem in their spot in the woods, Aleen's father came swinging, yelling about a man in the village who had told him his daughter was leaving with a boy and they had plans to never come back. And though Aleen looked at her father and stood her ground and shook her head and told him all the lies she could possibly tell him in the few moments it took him to move from their front door to her place at the table, still he raged. He smacked a fist into her jaw and sent her reeling back. He took another swing and another, knocking Aleen to the floor. She got back up. He did it again. She got back up. He did it once more, and this time she stayed down. He took out a rope and tied her to a chair. She could not even move.

Her father leaned close to her and said, "You will never leave." His breath smelled of onions. His eyes were hard black rocks. "You will never leave me. I will hunt this boy down. I will kill him."

"No, Father," she said. "Please."

He did not listen, of course. He was caught in a rage from which he could not escape. He stormed out of their cottage. Aleen shook the ropes, trying desperately to free herself. Her father did not know about her magic, and magic, fortunately, can slice a rope in two. So she stole away and ran faster than her father, all the way to the hill where Jem lived. She pounded on the door, hardly able to see, begging him to open it before her father reached him.

She fell into Jem's arms when he appeared behind the door.

"You must go," she said. "Without me. You must go now. My father is on his way. He knows."

Jem took her in his arms and looked out toward the village, where the flames were gathering. He looked back at Aleen, and took both her cheeks in his hands. "You will come with me," he said.

"No," she said. "I cannot. He will never stop until he finds you, and if I am there…" She pulled away from his arms. "Go. Without me. You must if you would keep your life."

"Perhaps I do not want my life without you," Jem said quietly.

Oh, Aleen loved this boy so much that she was willing to let him go, never to see him again, so he might simply live.

And yet Jem loved her enough to risk his life to take her with him.

What could these star-crossed lovers do?

But there was not enough time to consider it, for Aleen's father came crashing into the yard, with what seemed like the entire village behind him. His eyes turned confused and angry when he saw her guarding the door, but he stood surprised for only a moment. She glanced behind her. Jem had not fled. She could not let them past her. She would die before they got inside.

"You," her father said. "How did you get out?"

Aleen shook her head. Her father pointed a long, skinny

finger at her. "She is a sorceress," he said. "Seize her!" And the swarm of people moved forward, and then Jem jumped out from behind the door, and suddenly there were hands everywhere, scratching and pulling and she could not see where Jem had gone and then she closed her eyes and flicked her arm. Her basket hit the ground and lengthened into a staff. The people around her fell flat, and there was only her father, near Jem, his knife poised at Jem's throat.

"No, Father!" Aleen screamed. She could not keep the tears from falling. "Please, no. He will leave. He will never come back."

Her father looked at her with eyes that saw no reason. In fact, they saw nothing at all. "I cannot even trust my own daughter," he said in her general direction. He grabbed Jem's shirt and pulled him closer, and before Aleen could do anything, he drew the knife across her beloved's throat. Aleen screamed and closed her eyes, and the whole world shook.

When she opened her eyes again, her father was lying on the ground. She could see him breathing in great gasps, but she only had eyes for Jem. She rushed to Jem's side and knelt. He looked at her, his eyes growing glassy. His face was pale. Blood, everywhere.

"Oh, Jem," she said. "My love." She kissed him on the mouth. "I must make you vanish. It is the only way to save you."

He looked at her again, but his eyes were swiftly turning dark. Her staff hit the ground again. Where Jem had been there was nothing.

She felt the loss in the deepest places of her heart. He would not die, for a vanishing spell, timed at just the right moment, can save a life, though not many know this. He would merely reappear in some distant land as someone else, perhaps a man much older or much younger, with only a scar across his neck that could be easily hidden with the right kind of cloth, which is precisely what he would do. He would change his name and live his life and, for a time, search for her, but he would never see her again, until a day much, much later in time than any of them had ever thought possible.

She had lost. But he had lived.

Huntsman

A strange man occupies the castle steps when Sir Greyson makes his way back down the road from the village. He is a young man, dressed in what looks like armor, except painted brown and green and all the colors of the earth. Were he to stand in a forest, Sir Greyson is not sure anyone would even notice. His hair is the color of straw and hangs over one of his eyes and across his shoulders.

He rises to his feet when Sir Greyson nears. The man is tall, nearly as tall as Sir Greyson, but much younger than the captain. His brilliant blue eyes remind Sir Greyson of the color Fairendale's sky once wore. The man's eyes do not stay on Sir Greyson but flick, flick, flick, to every corner of the world, as if he is watching for something, waiting for something, searching for something, perhaps.

Sir Greyson reaches the castle steps and stops. "Do you need assistance?" the captain says. He assumes, you see, that the man used the iron knocker on the castle doors and no one answered, since this is what happened to him as well. But the boy called Garth flies out from the castle doors at precisely that moment. He screeches to a stop before the two men. "Captain," Garth says. "I did not know you had returned."

"I went to search the village," Sir Greyson says.

"To find the prince?" Garth says.

"Yes," Sir Greyson says. "Where is it you go?"

"To bid you return," Garth says. He nods toward the man. "There is a visitor, and King Willis, the Most High King, says he is vulnerable."

Sir Greyson tilts his head. Did the boy just say King Willis, the Most Wide King? Surely not. He searches the boy's face, but he cannot find a single sign of amusement there.

"Very well," Sir Greyson says. He looks at the man. "Follow me."

The men file in, moving in a single line, though the hallway is wide enough to permit forty men walking side by side. Sir Greyson follows Garth. The unknown man follows Sir Greyson. At the entrance to the throne room, Garth puts his hand on the door, but before he can pull it, Sir Greyson touches his shoulder. Garth turns.

"I thought no one else was here," Sir Greyson says.

"I remained," Garth says. "When no one else did." No one, that is, except for the boy Calvin. Garth's eyes fall to the floor. "For the king." It is untrue, of course. Garth remains for his brothers and sisters, who may very well be trapped in the dungeons beneath the dungeons. He has not yet found a way in, but he knows of the boy Calvin, who is charged with taking the children their allotted food for the day. The boy runs the kitchens now that Cook has disappeared. Garth is merely waiting for a chance to follow Calvin on his nightly adventure. Garth will find the dungeons beneath the dungeons. He will.

Sir Greyson removes his hand from Garth's shoulder. "I am sure the king is grateful for your service," he says.

"And yours as well," Garth says. He pulls open the doors and announces the captain and the visitor. The men move through the door and down the red carpet.

"Ah," King Willis says. "Captain. You have returned."

"With no good news, I fear," Sir Greyson says.

"You have searched the village, I presume?" King Willis says.

"Yes, sire," Sir Greyson says.

"And you have not found my son?" King Willis says.

"No, sire," Sir Greyson says.

"Blast," King Willis says. His hand drums against the golden arm of the throne, though even one who does not know King Willis as his captain does can see that he is not as concerned with this bit of news as he is the next.

"And the children?" King Willis says. "You found no sign of them?"

Sir Greyson was not aware that he should be looking. But nevertheless, he says, "No, sire."

"And who is this who waited on my steps?" King Willis says. "Who says he has some news for us?"

Sir Greyson extends an arm to the mysterious man, for he did not get the man's name.

"I am called the Huntsman," the man says.

"Ah," King Willis says. "A Huntsman. At precisely the right time. How fortunate."

Sir Greyson studies the man. Those blue eyes. They startle him every time he looks upon them, as if he has seen them before. As if they belong to someone else. But who? And how?

"And from where do you come?" King Willis says.

"Everywhere," the Huntsman says. "And nowhere."

"Come now," King Willis says. "Speak plainly to me. I was never one for riddles."

"It does not matter from where I come," the Huntsman says. "It matters only what I can do."

King Willis tilts his head. "Hunt," he says. "I am listening."

The Huntsman bows deeply to King Willis. "I would like to offer my services," he says. "I would like to help you hunt for the missing children."

The king looks at the Huntsman, but of course he does not really see the man. He sees only the glory that will come from finally catching the magic boy who dares threaten his throne. The king claps his hands, like a toddler who has just received a new toy. "Splendid," he says. "That is splendid."

Sir Greyson does not think this is splendid at all, for he has come with another request, one more entreaty for King Willis to set free the imprisoned children before the townspeople storm the castle and take them back. He knows where the children are. He does not know how to get them out, but he knows where they are, and this is, at least, a start. Surely the one hundred forty-three prophets trapped in the dungeons will be able to help put the last piece in place so the children might be freed.

This Huntsman has thrown a wrench in the plans.

"We have searched for the children everywhere," Sir Greyson says. "And we have found nothing. They are surely dead after the dragon fires. They could not escape where my men died."

"They are not dead," the Huntsman says. "They are alive and well." He looks at Sir Greyson and then at the king.

"And how could you know such a thing?" Sir Greyson says.

The Huntsman narrows his eyes at Sir Greyson. "I have my ways," he says.

"You know where they are," the king says, and it is not a question, merely a statement of fact, for he has heard the certainty in the Huntsman's voice. He has never known a man like this, only heard the stories told of them. They are said to track the wildest of prey to the very ends of the earth until they are cornered and helpless.

Yes. That is precisely what King Willis needs done.

And yet he hesitates. Yes, he has heard of the skill and determination of a Huntsman. But he has also heard their price.

"Yes," the Huntsman says. "I know where they are."

"And what is it you ask from me?" King Willis says. He leans back so the throne touches his shoulders. He knows, of course, that he will already pay whatever price this Huntsman names, for the children must be found and the throne must be secured.

"I ask only food and clothing and safety for my family," the Huntsman says.

"Your family?" King Willis says. He looks to the door of the throne room, as if a family might have followed the Huntsman inside the castle walls.

The Huntsman gives one short laugh. "My family is not here," he says. "They remain in the land from which I came."

"And what is that land, exactly?" Sir Greyson says, unable to trust this man.

But King Willis says, "Then consider it granted. Provided

you deliver me all the children."

"I will," the Huntsman says.

"Alive," the king says.

"Yes," the Huntsman says.

"I shall decide what to do with them when they stand before me and kneel," King Willis says.

"As you wish," the Huntsman says.

"Where might these children be, Huntsman?" Sir Greyson says.

The Huntsman turns to him, as if he has only just remembered that Sir Greyson still stands beside him. "They are in the Weeping Woods," he says. "Where they have been all along."

The room grows quiet. It is quite impossible. The woods were burned. The children would have died.

"All of them?" he says.

"All of them," the Huntsman says.

"I have no men to offer for protection," King Willis says.

The Huntsman flashes his teeth at the king. They are normal-looking teeth, though Sir Greyson has wondered, just now, if he is, in fact, human. He looks like a man. Talks like a man. Moves like a man. But there is something unnatural about him all the same. "I do not need men," the Huntsman says. "I need only food and some supplies."

"Consider it done," the king says, and he gestures to Sir Greyson. "My captain will take care of you."

Sir Greyson bows to King Willis and then turns on his heel. Just before they have reached the door, which stands open still, King Willis says, "How long, Huntsman?"

The Huntsman turns back. "How long, Your Majesty?"

"How long until you bring me the children?" King Willis says. "I am not a patient man."

"It is difficult to say," the Huntsman says. "A few days. Perhaps longer."

"My son," King Willis says. He rises from the throne. "What of him?"

"Your son," the Huntsman says. "He is missing."

"Yes," King Willis says, and his face folds a little. Sir Greyson, for the first time in perhaps his entire life, feels sorry for his king. "Might you find him, too?"

"He is safe," the Huntsman says.

"How could you possibly know?" Sir Greyson says. He is not able to keep the words from flying out of his mouth.

The Huntsman looks at him, and then away. "I watch," he says. "And no one sees." He looks at the king again and says, "I will find him after the other children, if you so desire it."

"Yes," King Willis says. "Thank you."

Sir Greyson does not think he has ever, in the history of the kingdom of Fairendale, heard King Willis say those two words. Ever. He stares at his king, marveling at this unexpected happenstance.

Perhaps there is hope for the kingdom yet. Perhaps there is a shred of humanity still living in King Willis. Perhaps they do not need a new king at all, only the transformation of an old one.

Sir Greyson follows the Huntsman out the front doors of the castle.

At his first opportunity, he breaks toward the village, never looking back.

We may look back, however. And what we see is this: the Huntsman, moving with unbroken steps toward the woods, as if he did not notice that another man ever walked beside him.

Quite fortunate for Sir Greyson, as I am sure we can all agree.

Maude and the hiding children work the land, as they were told by the Enchantress. They plant two vegetable gardens with the seeds the Enchantress gave them. Maude has made the house comfortable for the children—cramped, but comfortable. They are, after all, living in an old shoe that has been enlarged until it is hardly recognizable as a shoe. But it is a shoe all the same, with low ceilings and a tunnel up, used as a fireplace, and too many children tripping all over one another. If one could see invisible houses like this one, one would be quite impressed that inside are twelve rooms and a sitting area with a kitchen. Maude, now, breezes around in the kitchen, pulling a batch of cookies from the iron stove. The Enchantress has not been round to see them today, but Maude expects that she will. And because the Enchantress can never pass up one of her pumpkin spice cookies, this is what Maude has decided to bake today. It is her gift of sorts, in return for news of Hazel.

Truth be told, Maude and the children eat more food now than they ever did in the village. Might this flight have been good for them? It is impossible to tell as yet.

For now, Maude must grudgingly admit that it has been good for all of them, though the longing for Hazel and Arthur and Theo steal over her once the children have all been tucked in their beds.

And yet while they eat better than they have ever eaten before, the children are still forbidden to be free. They are trapped inside a shoe, for there are dangers waiting for them, dangers the Enchantress says will find them if they venture out. They can never know if others are watching, you see. So they remain inside, growing more frustrated by the day.

Maude finishes the cookies and moves to the next item on

the list she keeps inside her head, for she wants to move, always move. It is the only way she can keep from thinking of her daughter and her son and her husband. Today, she keeps herself from thinking by turning a bit of flour, pulled from the wheat in the hidden field, into loaves of bread for the children. There is nothing quite like the smell of fresh bread. The children could eat it for all the rest of their days. She suspects it reminds them of home, where the baker used to pass them hot morsels right out of the oven. Here they get whole loaves. This has been some consolation for the way they miss their families and their homes.

Maude kneads the bread and flips it over. She puts it in a pot and hangs it over the open fire. It is always better over the open fire.

And then there is nothing for her hands to do, and she broods. She broods about Arthur and the dragons. She broods about Theo and his disappearance. She broods about what her daughter could possibly offer the Enchantress. She pokes her head into the great room, where the children sit and talk and play. They have found a chair that one of the girls turned into a spinning wheel. They sit on it and spin, and then they try to walk. Maude watches them for a time. She smiles, in spite of her sadness and unrest. At least they seem happier here. At least there is that. This is what Hazel has done.

The ache returns to her chest in a fierce fire.

She returns to the kitchen and is startled to see the Enchantress there. The woman has the uncanny ability to move so silently that she appears to appear from nowhere. It is as if the Enchantress enjoys startling Maude. She smiles when Maude puts a hand to her chest.

"Enchantress," Maude says, trying to still her heart.

"I have news," the Enchantress says.

"My daughter?" Maude says. "Is she well?"

"Yes," the Enchantress says. "Your daughter is well. She is always well. She will never not be well." The Enchantress sweeps into the kitchen, her skirts brushing the doorway. "I must speak with you, away from the children."

"This way," Maude says, leading the Enchantress into her small chambers. Fear claws at the back of her throat. It must be bad news. She knew their safety was too good to be true. She knew this house was too good to be true. She knew they would be found sooner or later.

"Sit down," Maude says, and then she remembers her manners. "Would you care for a bit of tea?"

"No," the Enchantress says. "I have only come to talk."

"Pumpkin spice cookies?" Maude says. "They are freshly out of the oven."

The Enchantress hesitates. But then she says, "Perhaps on my way out." She gestures to the spot beside her on Maude's bed. "Please. Sit with me."

"What is it?" Maude says. "Tell me before I draw my own conclusions."

"There is news from the castle," the Enchantress says. "News of a Huntsman."

"A Huntsman," Maude says. No. Not a Huntsman. Not now, when they have only just settled into their new lives. Even a king would not stoop that low, would he? Would he? They are only words trapped in her mind, for fear keeps them locked. She can only, in truth, stare at the Enchantress with eyes wide and dark.

"Yes," The Enchantress says. "A Huntsman who is hunting the children."

Maude gasps and presses her hand to her mouth. "So we will be found after all," she says. "After all this work." She looks around the room, as if to find answers the walls cannot possibly hold.

"He knows you are in the woods," the Enchantress says. "He does not know precisely where. This enchantment is very powerful."

"Very well," Maude says. She knows there is more coming. She knows they are not safe at all.

"But we will have to do more," the Enchantress says.

"More," Maude says. It is as if she is a parrot, dear reader. This is what shock can do to people, you see. She has no ability to think for herself right now. She hopes only that the Enchantress will tell her what to do.

And the Enchantress does not disappoint. "We must move the children," she says.

"But we cannot move the children," Maude says. "This is their home now."

"We must," the Enchantress says. "If we want them to remain hidden. They must all separate."

Maude looks at the Enchantress, her eyes narrowed. "But they will not survive without me. Or Arthur…" She lets the name trail off. Tears fill her eyes. "No," she whispers.

She had not meant to say any of those words out loud.

"They will survive," the Enchantress says. "It is the only way." She looks toward the doorway. Maude does, too, but there are no children bursting through.

"It is the only way?" Maude says.

"Yes," the Enchantress says. "Even with all the enchantments I have placed on this house, it is only a matter of time. The Huntsman will find you."

"Very well," Maude says. "I see." She is babbling, for she does not know what to do with herself. And then she finds the words that matter now. "What shall we do?"

"Hazel will be fine," the Enchantress says, as though she has not heard Maude. "My magic is strong enough to keep one hidden. But these children."

"What shall we do, then?" Maude says again.

The Enchantress looks at Maude. She lets out a breath. "Have no fear," she says. "I shall take care of everything." She rises from her seat. She gives Maude a cold, long look that sends a shiver down Maude's back. "But you must trust me implicitly."

Maude does not know for sure if she can do this. The life of her daughter is in the hands of this woman, after all. Can she trust the Enchantress to protect Hazel? Can she trust the Enchantress to save the children where she cannot?

But what choice does she have, dear reader?

So Maude merely nods and looks the Enchantress full in the face. "Yes," she says. "I will trust you implicitly."

"Very well, then," the Enchantress says. And with a swish of her skirt, she is gone. Maude sits on the edge of her bed and ponders. Has she done the right thing?

The children giggle from the great room, and she returns to her post in the doorway, determined not to let them see just how much fear the Enchantress has brought in this visit and how drastically their lives will change in very little time. She has no need to burden them for now. They are children. Let them play. Let them be merry. Let them hold their happiness for a time.

Zorag has taken quite a liking to the human he has captured. He would very much like to keep him around, in fact. The man does not eat much, he is not too difficult to please, and he provides Zorag with fascinating conversation about kingdoms and travels and men. The man has finally stopped talking about war and children and has begun responding to the questions Zorag has about the things of greater interest to him, such as learning how the humans fare without the dragon riders they once had.

"Tell me how travel has changed," Zorag says now.

"I was not around when the people rode dragons to distant lands," Arthur says.

"Yes, but how has travel slowed now?" Zorag says.

"The people do not travel much anymore," Arthur says.

"In my time," Zorag says. "They traveled great distances in very little time."

"The people of Fairendale stay in Fairendale," Arthur says. "It is the way of things today."

"And how goes the trade?" Zorag says.

"Poor," Arthur says. "The only trade comes in from the Violet Sea, if it is permitted by the creatures below water. No man can risk the long trip on land, through the Weeping Woods, except for the king's soldiers." Arthur looks toward Fairendale.

"And the king cannot spare his soldiers."

"So the people," Zorag says. "What do they do for food?"

Arthur traces a pattern in the dirt. "They starve," he says.

"No," Zorag says. "They cannot starve. The kingdom must feed its people."

Arthur looks at the dragon's golden eyes. He feels an ache inside his belly. He is hungry, but he dares not ask for anything. "It is much different in the kingdom of Fairendale than it was in your time," Arthur says. He squints at the dragon lands. "Much harsher."

"I have come to understand this," Zorag says. "A king who hunts children rules the land." His rumble has turned gentle, as if he is remembering better days. "Tell me about the magic that has set a king on the hunt."

"There is said to be a boy," Arthur says. "A boy with magic."

"A boy with magic," Zorag says. "Who may steal a throne."

"It is said," Arthur says, but he does not say much more, for he cannot risk revealing to this dragon that the very boy he mentions is his beloved son.

"And is this boy a kind boy?" Zorag says.

"There is no boy with magic," Arthur says. So long has he told this tale, you see, that the words come out almost automatically, as if he has no control over whether or not truth passes his lips.

"There is a boy with magic," Zorag says. His growl carries an edge. He is not pleased that Arthur would do him this disservice, which is precisely what telling a lie is—a disservice to the person to whom one tells it. People like knowing the truth. And what would Zorag do to harm this magical child who has gone missing?

Arthur is a wise man. He knows what has upset the dragon. And so he says, "Yes, there is a boy with magic." And then he goes a step deeper. "He is my son."

"Your son?" Zorag says. He turns his magnificent face toward Arthur. Heat from his mouth warms Arthur's skin, as a fire might when one is standing a safe distance away.

"Yes," Arthur says. "My son."

"Your son would be king, and you are running?" Zorag says. His eyes grow more golden, glowing in the shifting darkness.

"Yes," Arthur says. "It is safer this way."

"Safer, perhaps," Zorag says. "But is it better?" He does not even notice, dear reader, that he has ventured into the very territory he has wanted to avoid all of these days: the idea of overthrowing a kingdom. Zorag, you see, longs for the days when a king loved the dragons, when the people of Fairendale needed them, when dragons had a purpose and companionship and humans who trusted them. This longing is what has circled his thoughts to what might have been.

"Your son," Zorag says. "He is a good boy?"

"Always," Arthur says. "He has a kind heart. A true heart. A noble heart."

"And he would not lose that heart were a kingdom placed in his hands?" Zorag says, for he must be certain. One can never know what one will do when power is handed to them. But if one has a kind and true and noble heart, power cannot make it easily stray.

"No," Arthur says. "I do not believe he would. Theo is…" Arthur lets the sentence dangle off. Zorag waits, but Arthur does not speak again.

"He is different from the king who rules the land now," Zorag says, for he has somehow understood what Arthur meant to say. "He is different from the prince who will inherit it all."

"The prince," Arthur says. "The prince and his father are only misguided. That is all."

"You say that about the very ones who would steal your son and kill him so they might keep a throne?" Zorag says. His growl remains soft, gentle.

"Yes," Arthur says. "They do not know what they do."

"And how is it you know this?" Zorag says.

Arthur looks at the dragon and then down at the ground. He has traced a pattern around the rock, a wide oval rut that swallows his finger. "I know the stories," he says. "About an enchanted throne." And the look Arthur turns on Zorag is so terribly sad that Zorag cannot bring himself to ask any more, though he wonders, as you might wonder, about this enchanted throne. What is its story? How did it come to the kingdom of Fairendale? What power does it hold over our king and prince?

Arthur is not quite ready to tell this story, dear reader. And so we, too, must wait.

"Your son," Zorag says after a time. "If we were to find him, he would inherit the throne?"

"It would mean a fight," Arthur says. "But he has the gift of magic."

"And he is alive still?" Zorag says.

This is something Arthur has not considered as yet. He has not allowed himself to consider it, in truth. The possibility that Theo could be dead is a possibility Arthur cannot bear to consider, you see.

"Yes," Arthur says. "I hope."

"You do not know where he is?" Zorag says.

"No," Arthur says. "He never wanted the throne. He might have fled quite far from these lands to escape it."

Zorag bends his head so he is eye to eye with Arthur. "Tell me about your son."

"He is a good boy. Strong. Courageous," Arthur says. "Always searching for the ones who live in need. Always giving what he has so that others may live."

Zorag lifts his head again, gazing out upon the lands of Fairendale. They have begun to wither. This has not escaped him. "He sounds like a boy I once knew," Zorag says.

Arthur stares at his hands. "Who was the boy you once knew?" he says.

"Just a boy," Zorag says. Just a boy he loved. He does not say this last part aloud, of course, for Zorag does not want Arthur to know yet that he ever loved a human. He does not tell Arthur that this boy would have once made an honorable king, if the evil one had not banished him from the land. He does not reveal that he once had a rider who was bound to him forever, but the rider vanished on the heels of a spell.

He does not say that he has looked long and hard for that boy, and he has never found him.

Zorag breathes fire toward Fairendale. Arthur scrambles to his feet. He has no notion what might have caused the dragon sudden anger, but he is wise enough to know he must get out of the way. He slips behind a rock.

"Come," Zorag says. "I lost myself for a moment."

Arthur emerges from behind the rock.

Zorag's head hovers above him, so Arthur must look up to meet those golden eyes. "If we found your boy," Zorag says. "Perhaps the kingdom could become what it once was."

"Perhaps," Arthur says.

"Perhaps the dragons would resume their rightful place alongside the humans, living in peace and love," Zorag says.

"Perhaps," Arthur says once more.

Zorag huffs. "It is only that we are not strong enough for a battle," he says. It is as if he is trying to talk himself out of helping Arthur, dear reader. "We must not get involved in a battle."

"But there will be a battle, regardless," Arthur says. "The people will not simply hand over their children to the king. Even now, they are likely planning their war." Arthur, of course, has no idea whether this is true. But he has seen his opportunity. And he will take it.

"We must keep the treaty," Zorag says. "We must remain in our lands."

"Very well," Arthur says, for he knows he cannot sway the mind of this dragon.

"And yet," Zorag says, and Arthur feels a warm hope rise in his chest. Those two words, dear reader. They are magical ones. "You must find your son."

"Yes," Arthur says.

"If we search, we shall not be able to keep the treaty," Zorag says. "It will be dangerous work."

"Perhaps," Arthur says.

Zorag looks on Arthur. His eyes glow in the dark. "You do not know where your son may be?" he says.

"No," Arthur says.

Zorag falls quiet again. And then he straights, his head rising to a place well above Arthur's head.

"They broke the treaty first." At first, Arthur mistakes the words for Zorag's. But then Zorag's cousin emerges from shadows, his black body nearly invisible in the dark. Only his red eyes give clue that he is there.

Arthur feels a cold finger stroke his back. Blindell will ruin it all. He has seen the exchanges between Zorag and Blindell. Zorag believes his cousin is too rash, too intent on revenge. Arthur, in truth, has thought much the same. Arthur turns around to face the dragon. Blindell is pointing one talon in Arthur's direction, as if Arthur takes on the full brunt of guilt for crossing into the lands of Morad and breaking the treaty. But all he can do is wait for Zorag to respond.

Zorag lets out a long breath, as if he has already grown weary of this exchange. He is, in fact, weary. He is weary of trying to decide what is best for his land. He is weary of wondering what he might do to restore the kingdom of Fairendale, which he loves still. He is weary of this sad man, who has ceased to eat most days. The human will die of starvation, but not because the dragons do not feed him.

He is weary of feeling torn, wanting to keep his dragons safe and yet wanting to help the man and so help all the land.

He must not risk any more lives. The dragons risked much in the Great Battle, and look where it got them. Zorag growls in frustration.

"We cannot," he says. "We cannot bring a war on the land."

"We will all die soon if we remain chained here in this land without food," Blindell says. "The dragons once had free reign." He points a talon toward Arthur again. "He says that can happen again."

"Yes, it could," Arthur says, so softly the dragons almost do not hear him. "My son would make it better."

At precisely this moment, two more dragons drop to the ground before them, a red one who breathes smoke as she huffs and a blue one who shimmers in the moonlight even when he is still.

The red one looks at Zorag with tender eyes.

"Malera," he says. "Why are you here?"

"We come to counsel," Malera says. "We come to talk about what Blindell has told us." She looks at Arthur. "With the human."

"And what is it my cousin has told you?" Zorag says.

"He has told us everything," says the other dragon. His blue scales shimmer again. A green horn sits on the top of his face, right between his green eyes that match exactly the undersides of his wings, though one could not tell in this darkness what colors he wears. Arthur has seen him about during the day. He is the most beautiful of the dragons, the one who brings him food most often, terrifying when one first looks upon him, for his teeth show from the sides of his cheek, but Arthur has come to trust him in the days since his captivity. This dragon would not harm him. Of that he is certain.

"Larus," Zorag says. "You as well? You have all come to tell me I am wrong to desire peace?"

"Something must be done," Larus says. "We are starving. We will die whether we fight or not. At least if we fight we have the opportunity to change whether we live or die."

"But I never wanted a war," Zorag says. "I never wanted to fight."

"Sometimes wars come to us even when we are not looking," Malera says. "Your father told me that once."

Yes, Zorag remembers his father saying that. His father. Oh, how he misses his father. Erell would know exactly what to do. He would lead the dragons with authority and strength and confidence. Zorag fears he does not carry any of those virtues anymore, for he has never ruled his people in any time other than this one. This time when dragons are forbidden to leave the lands of Morad. How easily authority and strength and confidence can leak from a leader when he finds himself subjugated.

Malera waddles closer to Zorag. "Besides," she says. "They are children."

She looks at Arthur. Arthur turns his gaze to her, and he cannot help nodding his head, agreeing with her, for it is true. They are only children. Innocent children caught in a war they did not ask to begin.

"What if his son could change our futures?" Larus says. "What if he could set us back in our proper places, with the freedom we once had?"

"Serving the people?" Blindell growls. His eyes turn hard. "You would call that freedom?"

"You speak of what you do not know," Larus says.

"I would never serve the people," Blindell says. "Never again. Our proper place is roaming the lands, wherever we would go."

"We were never subject to the people," Malera says. "We were bound in friendship and peace and love."

Blindell does not say anything more, but Zorag knows his cousin. He can tell Blindell did not plan on this turn of events. He is not a dragon keen on helping people, and perhaps this is what gives Zorag a momentary surge of knowing. He must show his cousin how beautiful the land used to be.

And so he says, "Very well. We shall do what needs to be done."

There is, perhaps, no one quite as happy as Arthur is this moment, anywhere in the world. They shall find his family. They shall protect the people. They shall save his son.

"Call the rest of the council," Zorag says to Blindell. "We shall make our plans."

Blindell takes to the sky, and Arthur watches him until he has vanished in a patch of black.

Freedom

Aleen's father did not live long after Jem disappeared. A man full of anger and hatred and the need for control does not make many friends, and Aleen suspected that the innkeeper had poisoned his drinks. The innkeeper was an old man who would often walk by her house and look for her, not out of curiosity but out of concern, judging by the sharp gaze that softened each time it met hers. She would stand by the window and wave, a prisoner in her own home. She had not fought it this time, though. Her heart had died when Jem left.

So Aleen did not grieve all that much when her father dropped dead one day and she found herself quite unexpectedly free. She could move about as much as she desired. She could lift her face to the sunny sky and smell the wind and touch the trees behind which she and Jem had hidden during their evening meetings so watching eyes would not see the magic they practiced. Someone's eyes had watched, though. She had never discovered whose.

Aleen had not been free for long before she caught the eye of one of the village men. Perhaps it was her dark, exotic skin, or her even darker eyes. Perhaps it was the stories people told of her, in which she sounded mysterious and a bit frightening. Perhaps he wanted to discover how much of what was said about this woman was true. At any rate, he approached her in the village streets.

"Aleen," he said.

She had been walking home. She turned and met his eyes, soft green and clear, like the foliage of White Wind's evergreens. She did not trust many men, after her father. One man had told of her plans with Jem, after all. And another had beaten her and tied her up. A woman who has been through such betrayal does not trust easily.

But Aleen looked into the heart of this man before her, and she saw that it was good.

"Yes," she said, as if agreeing with what her heart told her.

"I am Milton," the man said. He stuck out his hand. It was large and hairy. Aleen stuck her own small hand in his. His skin was softer than she had imagined. "I am pleased to make your acquaintance finally."

"The pleasure is mine," Aleen said. They bowed to each

other. Milton did not let go of her hand.

"I would like to ask your permission to call on you," Milton said.

Aleen dipped her head. "I should like that very much," she said.

For weeks he knocked on her door and they would stroll through the village, until one day he asked if she would care to sup with him, and she said yes. They ate a humble dinner of broth and bread down at the innkeeper's place. He told her that he was not a man of wealth, but he was a man of integrity. He would give her a quiet home and love her well. She could see that already.

"I have watched you for some time," Milton said. "You are very sad."

Aleen dropped her eyes. "Not so sad that I can never be happy again," she said, though she wondered if it was true.

"I would like to try to make you happy again," Milton said. "I would like you to be my wife."

Aleen inclined her head toward him. "I would very much like that," she said.

He was not Jem, of course. But Aleen soon grew to love Milton, in a very different way, like a friend. They married on a sunny winter morning while the townspeople looked on.

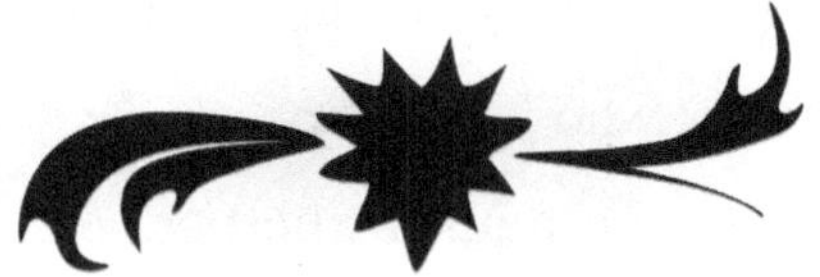

Decisions

Standing in his throne room, alone, without even the company of his page, King Willis thinks. And when King Willis thinks, at least when he thinks without the help of the magic mirror propped a few paces from the throne and, now, covered with its scarlet curtain, he sometimes gets ideas. But the ideas of King Willis do not always make sense, as is the case with this one that has popped quite forcibly into our king's brain.

He will ride to the village.

Yes, he will ride to the village.

He will command the people to let his son go. Surely that will work. Surely, once they see their king making an effort, they will know that they should not dare cross him. He is their king, after all. He is their ruler.

So though King Willis has never saddled a horse himself, though he has never, in truth, ridden a horse at all, he pulls one from the stables, buckles the saddle as best he can figure and climbs on. It takes him five tries, dear reader, to swing one leg over the horse, and he nearly gives up before that final time. But then the leg catches, and King Willis is able to slide himself atop the back of the horse, who is none too pleased, truth be told.

King Willis flicks the reins, as he has seen Sir Greyson do, and the horse begins forward, groaning with every step, for King Willis, remember, is a heavy man. He is not so heavy as he was days ago, since Cook has disappeared, but he is heavy all the same.

The village people have never seen King Willis on a horse. They have never seen him in the village, either. They hear the horse's steady steps, from their place beneath the ground, but what they hear more is the groan of his horse. And this is what causes them to grow silent and turn their eyes upon Sir Greyson, who has only just told them about the Huntsman.

They do not emerge from their secret hiding, however, for they want nothing of what waits for them outside this magical door. And, besides, this place must remain secret.

Were it Queen Clarion who had traveled this road, it might, perhaps, have written a quite different story. The people might have eased her heart a bit. They might have made their demands in a gentler, kinder way. But Queen Clarion has taken to her bed, much like many of these parents took to theirs after their own children were stolen from them. She will not remain there, of course, but we must, for now, allow a mother her grief.

"Someone is coming," Sir Greyson says.

The people suck in their breaths. "Who?" Cora says.

Sir Greyson shakes his head. "I do not know," he says. "But I will go."

"I shall go with you," Cora says. She turns to the people. "Stay here. Remain as quiet as you can." The people nod, and Sir Greyson and Cora emerge through the secret door before the rider, who travels slower than any rider they have ever seen, can draw close enough to see them.

Sir Greyson meets his king in the middle of the village, his face a study in confusion. "Sire?" he says, and the word comes out as a question. "To what do we owe the pleasure of your visit?" Sir Greyson looks behind him, but Cora is not there, though she followed him out.

"I come to take back my son," the king says.

Sir Greyson thinks that the king has, perhaps, gone mad. Why would the people hand over the prince simply because the king came for a visit? It is plain to see that the king cannot do much in the way of defending himself. He would not be able to dismount from the horse without an extra hand.

The captain shakes his head as much to clear the confusion as to understand this rash and foolish plan of the king's. "But you have their children," he says.

"Yes, yes, I know," King Willis says. "But I am the king." He lifts his head and squares his shoulders but cries out in pain. It is not so easy to ride a horse when one is so large. He shifts again. "I demand that they let my son go. I demand that they help me find their children."

"Help you find their children?" Sir Greyson says. "But you have the Huntsman."

"I would like to speak to the people," the king says. His eyes do not look so sad anymore. They look more confident, more resolved, perhaps, with a side of anger flickering deep. "I would like to lay out my plan."

"You shall speak to me," says a voice behind Sir Greyson. He knows without turning that it is Cora. "I speak for the people of this village."

"You," the king says, and he chuckles a little. "But you are a woman. Women do not lead villages."

The king is dismissive, as if he cannot fathom a world in which a woman could possibly speak for an entire village. Sir Greyson turns his eyes on Cora. Hers flash with anger, that same green he saw years ago when he told her he would join the king's army as commander and chief. Captain. He betrayed her then. He would not betray her now.

"I speak for the people," Cora says once more. "You speak

to me."

"Very well, then," King Willis says. "I do not expect you to understand plans as involved as these."

"I understand more than you know," Cora says.

"Unhand my son," the king says.

"No," Cora says. She folds her arms over her chest, the neck of her peasant dress puckering a bit. And even with all the dirt that marks her face and the dress that flows in tatters around her and the tangled hair lifted by the wind—perhaps because of it—she still appears formidable. Frightening, even. Intimidating. The king does not dismount from his horse, for he does not quite know how. But he has always enjoyed looking down on people, and the top of a horse's back provides him the surest opportunity of that.

"We will not give you your son until you give us our children," Cora says.

"Then you will lose your lives," the king says.

"And who will do that work for you, pray tell?" Cora says. Her eyes flash and churn.

"My captain," King Willis says. "He knows precisely what I intend to do." The king looks at Sir Greyson and then points at Cora. "Seize her, Captain."

Sir Greyson stands for a moment, caught in the middle of both. He looks from Cora to King Willis and back again. Cora's eyes hold a challenge. *Will you do what he says?* hers say. *Will you betray me again?*

The king expects that his captain will do what he says, for this is nothing less than what Sir Greyson has always done.

"Run," Sir Greyson murmurs to Cora, for this would make it easier. "Run."

"No," she says. "I will not run."

He should have known she would put him in such a position as this. After all, she did the very same thing fifteen years ago, when he loved her and she might have loved him and then he signed up for the king's guard because his father had left it in his hands. Sir Greyson looks from Cora, this woman he still loves, back to his king, and he does not know what to do.

Poor Sir Greyson. He does not know what to do, for he is an honorable man, and though he made a decision hours ago, to help the people, he is now in the presence of his king, this man he has served for fifteen years. Could there be some good left in the king? Could it be Sir Greyson who discovers it? Might King Willis deserve another chance, and another, and another? Sir Greyson knows that power can turn men into beasts. He knew King Willis when he was younger, when he was different. And this memory, today, is what makes it so difficult to decide what it is he should do. The people deserve their children. The king might very well deserve another chance. But who might draw out the good in King Willis?

"Sire," Sir Greyson says. "Sire, please. Let her go."

"This woman will not hand over my son," the king says. "She dares defy her king." The king's eyes darken, like black marbles in a puffy face. "Why else are you here?"

Sir Greyson, of course, cannot answer that very loaded question. He cannot explain that he has just exited the villagers' secret hiding place, where he tended to his mother and shared news about the Huntsman and drew up some plans for rescuing the children in the dungeons beneath the dungeons. The king would not understand. Of course he would not. He is driven by another concern: to find his son and the missing children.

King Willis shouts his orders again. "Seize her, Captain!" In truth, the look on Cora's face summons rage from the pit of his stomach. That woman—a woman!—dares defy his orders. She will pay. She will sit in the dungeons beneath the dungeons along with all the rest. Or perhaps another dungeon entirely, for he would not want her unintentionally reunited with her child, if she has one. King Willis looks into the hard, cold eyes of the woman and feels his chest grow hot with hate. Why is Sir Greyson hesitating? Why does he not grab her while she is near him?

"We can work this out, sire," Sir Greyson says, holding one hand up, looking from Cora to King Willis. "We do not need violence."

King Willis looks closely at Sir Greyson. His eyesight is not so keen, but it is plain to even him that his captain loves this maddening woman. His man's face is creased and tortured. Love has made the captain weak, and King Willis will not stand for it.

We know, dear reader, that love does not, in fact, make a person weak but much, much stronger, for it stretches and swells and opens a heart wide enough to see all the good in a world. But King Willis was taught otherwise in his earliest days, and so he does not quite know how to love well. Can you imagine a life without love? It is a wretched one, to be sure. King Willis is only beginning to feel the smallest bit of love for his son, which is what has brought him here, to this exact place in time.

"You," King Willis says. "You love her."

Sir Greyson looks behind him, back at Cora. Then he meets the eyes of his king.

"No," Sir Greyson says. He would try to deny it, but his king has already seen all he needs to see. He brings his horse closer to the man who is no longer his man, and he speaks his words so the woman may hear as well. "You will both pay," he says. "You will pay with your lives for this betrayal. I shall not forget." He turns and gallops as fast as his horse can gallop, which is more like a rapid walk for a poor horse carrying so much weight. The horse's legs buckle at every step, and it is quite comical to see, though Cora and Sir Greyson notice nothing.

When he is gone from their hearing, Cora says, "Well. At least you are done with that."

But Sir Greyson knows he is not done with that at all. He will not be done with it until the king has repaid him for what he has done.

Cora takes his hand. Hers is cold in his, and he feels no warmth left in his body.

Honor used to be his warmth. And he has just given away his honor for the woman and the village he loves.

But perhaps it is not as black and white as he believes.

At this point in our story, you might be wondering what has happened to Prince Virgil. I shall tell you straight away. Our prince lies on a cot, beneath the village fountains, guarded by the people inside, in the case that someone who was not invited down here steps through these secret doors. The people wait for Cora and Sir Greyson to return. The prince sleeps.

And what might come as quite some surprise is that our prince does not sleep as he would in his bed. The prince, you see, wears feathers now. He would be horrified, perhaps, to see himself in a mirror, for he has become the very bird said to have killed his grandfather. He has become a blackbird. A blackbird who sleeps.

Who has done such magic in this village?

Well, now, that is quite a mystery. If you remember, parents give up their gift of magic for children, and all the people gathered beneath this ground are parents.

But there is one who defies all the rules.

Wait. No. There are two.

One in the village and one in the castle, waiting for her time to come.

Maude tells the children about the Huntsman over dinner. She tells them that they must leave soon, separate. She tells them that they have all the provisions they could need, that the Enchantress has worked everything out so that they might live. But still the children cry. Still they shake. Still they worry.

It is true that some of their sadness can be found in leaving this home that is a shoe. You see, they have never had full bellies as they have had in the days since walking in this door with a knob like the knot of a shoelace. They have never slept as well, either. Their beds are soft and warm, and now Maude tells them they must give it all up? That they will not carry on together?

"I do not want to go," says a boy named Jasper.

"We must," Maude says. "It is the only way."

"I will not leave," says a girl named Ruby.

Maude touches the girl's dark red hair. "Hazel did not sacrifice so that we could be found, my dear," she says. She is surprised that her voice does not break. "Go. Pack your things. Dress warm."

"But what will we do?" Ursula says. Maude has waved them out of the kitchen, bid them go pack so they might be ready for the call that will come soon.

"The Enchantress has promised to take care of everything," Maude says.

And so the children begin their preparations, packing everything they might carry in knapsacks Maude made out of old towels she found in the kitchen, left for her by the Enchantress, and some out of old clothes the children had worn until they were only rags.

They are finished before Maude expects, and they gather in the great room.

"Why must we separate?" Jasper says. "Why must we go alone?"

"It is what the Enchantress says is best," Maude says. "She has seen it in her looking ball."

"We cannot separate," says a boy named Chester, who looks

exactly like his twin brother, Charles. "We are brothers."

"You must separate," Maude says. "That is the most important instruction the Enchantress gave me." She looks at the two boys.

"No," Chester says, grabbing his brother's hands.

Maude kneels before them. "I know it is difficult," she says. "I know love does not make leaving one another easy. But if you truly love one another, you must go your separate ways. It is for your safety. Sometimes love asks you to leave, because it is what is best. It is what keeps you both alive." She is thinking, of course, about her family, separated at every turn.

The two boys look at one another. Tears well in their eyes. "We have never been apart," Chester says.

"We will find each other again," Charles says. "We always do."

And it is true. The boys have always found each other. When they were younger and enjoyed wandering in the fields that lie to the north of Fairendale, between the village and the woods, they always wound up back at each other's side.

"We will know where others have gone?" Ursula says.

Maude shakes her head. "No," she says. "You must not."

"But how will we get where we are going?" Jasper says.

"The Enchantress," Maude says.

Truth be told, she does not entirely know how it is the

children will escape this time. She knows only that the Enchantress has asked for her trust. And Maude will readily give it, for it is the only way she may ever see her daughter again.

The children grow silent. Ursula notices that Maude does not have a knapsack. "Where is your bag, Mother Maude?" Ursula says. "Why do you have none?"

All eyes turn to Maude. She looks at her feet. "I need nothing," she says. "For I am not going."

"You are not going?" Ruby says. Her voice sounds like a wail, except it is soft.

"No," Maude says. She looks up now, beyond the faces of all these children, toward the place where she knows the house of the Enchantress to be, though there is no window through which she could see it. "I will stay with my daughter."

"But they will find you," says the girl called Thumbelina. "And then what will they do?"

It is not something Maude has let herself consider, for she is concerned only with staying near to her daughter. She shakes her head. "It matters not. I must be here." Maude claps her hands. "Now, children. It is time to go."

The Enchantress, on a late morning visit, laid out her plans for this evening in quite intricate detail, which is precisely the kind of plans Maude prefers. The Enchantress, however, did not tell everything, for she said magic must keep its secrets. The woman reviewed the children's time of departure many times, for it is the most important part.

Maude herds the children out the door. The girls carry their staffs in one hand and their knapsacks in another. The boys carry only their sacks. "Not too far," Maude says. "We must wait for the Enchantress." It is a powerful spell that hides this house, but if they venture too far, they walk outside the spell and will be seen clearly by anyone passing. They have not seen many pass these woods, but now with a Huntsman on the loose, they do not know what waits behind even a tree or a blade of grass. They have never seen a Huntsman. They do not know what a Huntsman looks like.

Fortunately, our Huntsman is not anywhere near the invisible houses just yet.

"What do we do?" Ursula says.

"Now we must wait," Maude says, though she cannot remember how long they must wait before she is to take them back inside and hide them all as well as she can. She does not remember how many minutes would pass before she could deem the plan of the Enchantress a failure. She watches the woods. The children fan out around her.

Ursula grabs Maude's hand. "I do not want you to stay here," Ursula says. "It is too dangerous."

Maude looks down at the child. Her thick black hair does

not move, for there is no wind today. "I will be safe," Maude
says.

"They will find you," Chester says. "They will take you
away."

"They will never find me," Maude says. "The Enchantress
has powerful magic."

"Then why must we leave?" Ursula says. "If her magic is so
powerful."

"The Huntsman is not searching for me," Maude says. "He
is searching for all of you."

"And a Huntsman only finds what he is looking for," Charles
says.

"So he will not find you," Chester says.

"No," Maude says. "He will not find me."

We can never truly know what may happen in our futures,
dear reader. Whether someone will be able to find us or whether
they will miss our presence entirely. I believe you may have
learned this truth in a game played in your time. Hide and Seek,
is it? One hides, another seeks, but the one hiding cannot know
whether the one seeking will find them or walk on by. It is part
of the thrill, perhaps. But for Maude, it is not a thrill at all. It is
only a cold terror that she tries to ignore.

Maude kisses all the children in turn.

"I will let you know when it is safe to return to this land,"

Maude says. This promise is not a promise she can make, in truth. But she does so anyway, for sometimes terrifying circumstances call for rash promises.

"And we will able to find you again," Jasper says. "We will be able to find you again when you call us home?"

Maude touches his long nose and looks in his sharp eyes. "Yes," she says. "Of course."

Though what she wants to say is that this silly shoe is not a home. It was never intended to be a home. Their home is back in the village, and they may never, ever see their homes again.

But she remains silent, for she does not want the children to worry more than they already do.

When she has finished saying goodbye to all the children in the line, Maude turns back to the woods and says, "Now. We must wait."

No one says another word. They all simply turn toward the east and wait for the Enchantress to come shimmering out of the woods with news of what comes next in this story.

They wait for far too long.

Arthur did not expect Zorag today. But the dragon drops from the sky with a thunderous shake before him, along with all the rest.

"It is time?" Arthur says.

Zorag's voice rumbles the ground. "No," he says. "It will be some time before we can do all that we have planned to do."

"Yes," Arthur says. "I understand." He looks out across the dragon lands, caught in twilight yet again. It is a quite magical time, when shadows might not be shadows at all and a sky glows with the last light of day. "I understand it takes time for a thing like this to come about."

"It could very well be months," Zorag says.

"I believe we have months," Arthur says. "I believe it will not be too late."

"And the rest of the children?" Zorag says. "What of them?"

"My wife will keep them safe," Arthur says. "She is a wise woman." He hesitates. "But perhaps I might visit."

"No," Zorag says. "There is no time. We must get started immediately."

"Yes. Very well," Arthur says, though he is, in truth, disappointed. He would like nothing more than to see his wife again, to reassure himself that the children are, in fact, safe. Mostly he would like Hazel and Maude to know that he did not die. But he cannot ask the dragons for this favor.

Zorag crouches before Arthur and bends his head to touch the ground. Arthur climbs on his back, marveling at the feel of

Zorag's scales on the palms of his hands. He knew this once, a very long time ago. He was just a boy when he felt the smooth, dry coolness of scales beneath his hands. When he knew what it was to fly.

Larus and Malera and Blindell watch the man and the dragon before them.

"Fly fast, Cousin," Blindell says. His black eyes flash. "Fly safe. I will tend to the land while you are gone."

"We will tend to the land," Larus says.

Zorag looks at Larus. "I know you will," he says. "And I will return with a greater army than you have ever seen take to the sky."

Arthur pats the dragon's back, a signal that he is ready, and Zorag lifts into the sky. His wings beat quickly, taking them up, up, up, but not quite so far up that Arthur does not see another shadow emerge from the dragons below. It appears to be a person. How is it that another person might live in the dragon lands, in his very own cave, and he, Arthur, missed it? He shakes his head, clearing his vision, and when he looks down again, the shadows have all vanished.

Arthur holds on with every muscle he has in his body. He is not used to flying, but comfort will come in time. Arthur lies flat on the dragon's back and closes his eyes so as not to look on the abandoned woods and its cracked trees that have, in fact, begun to revive themselves after the dragon's fire. But Arthur does not see it. He only sees black and the memory of another flight, made in a twilight long ago.

Had he looked, dear reader, he might have seen a line of children outside a patch of wood. He might have seen a man headed straight for that line, as if he, too, could see right through the invisible spell. He might have seen his daughter rush from another home.

Then again, the scene is cloaked behind a spell. So perhaps he would have seen nothing at all.

Gift

Ten years after her marriage, one week after her husband's death, the town prophet came knocking on Aleen's door.

Aleen did not know the town prophet. He was an old man who lived on a hill. The villagers called him a hermit, for they did not see him often, and, when they did, he merely mumbled his greetings and kept his eyes on the ground. Aleen thought him quite strange, though Jem had spoken well of him.

She was surprised to see him at her door, this man who had taught Jem magic.

"Aleen," he said. He had several teeth missing, and the ones that were still inside his mouth were crooked and yellow. He smelled of rosemary. "I have come to see you, Aleen."

She looked at him, alarmed that he appeared to desire entrance into her home, and then, deciding that she could not be hurt by a man so old as this, she opened the door wider. He came inside.

"Please, sit," she said, gesturing to a chair in the kitchen. "Would you care for some peppermint tea?"

"Courteous, too," he said, as if to himself. And then to her: "Yes, please. I thank you."

Aleen turned to the stove, her back toward him. She gazed out the window while she filled the kettle with water and hung it over the fireplace. It would squeal when it was fully boiled.

"I have come to see you," the old prophet said. "They call me Bregdon."

"Yes," she said, turning back around. She looked at his yellowish eyes. They were green in the middle. "I know."

He cackled for a moment, and then he stopped as abruptly as he had begun. "I have Seen something," he said.

Her heart slammed against the sides of her chest. She had only ever known this prophet to prophesy destruction and darkness in the land of White Wind. What could he have Seen that concerned her?

"Do not worry," the prophet said. "It is not what you think. I have come to you with a proposition."

She sat down across from him. Her hands, under the table, squeezed together. What could he want from her?

"Yes?" she said. "What is it?"

Bregdon's eyes grew serious. She noticed that they were the

deepest green she had ever seen, like the color of the white-capped evergreens in the woods surrounding White Wind. "You shall be with child," he said.

"A baby," she said. Her heart fluttered.

"Yes," he said. "A girl."

"A daughter," she said. And while she was as excited as any other mother would be upon the news of a child, Aleen also knew what it meant. The powers of magic passed to children, and a parent could never practice magic again. Not that she did much practicing here in White Wind. Only once in a while, when she burned a loaf of bread and turned it edible again, or when she could not reach one of the bowls her husband had put up too high, or when she did not feel so much like dusting the shelves of her cottage. She supposed she could give that up. For a baby?

"Ah," Bregdon said. "I see you know what this means for your magic."

Aleen nodded. "Yes," she said. "I do."

"There is another way," Bregdon said. "You do not have to lose your magic entirely. There is another way."

"What way?" she said. She had never heard of another way.

"The way of the prophet," he said.

"What do you mean?" Aleen said. "I have never heard of this way."

The prophet spread his hands on the table before her. They were wrinkled and spotted and jagged with bones. On his right pointer finger, he wore a golden ring. "Before a baby is conceived, one can choose to become a prophet and still live with a small gift of magic."

"A small gift of magic?" Aleen said. "But I have no need. My husband is dead. I shall not have a child, and if I do, it would already be too late."

"I have seen what is to come," Bregdon said. "I have seen a child."

Aleen stared at the prophet. A child. She had always wanted a child. "And I could keep some of my magic?" she said.

"Yes," Bregdon said. "A small gift. Something like Seeing the future. Or, perhaps, Seeing into a heart." He tilted his head. Of course he would have known.

"And what would I do with this magic?" Aleen said.

"Protect," Bregdon said. "And instruct, perhaps." He reached into his tunic and drew out a large book. She had thought him only stout, but it was a book that puffed his belly all this time. He placed it on the table. "There is more," he said, opening the book to a page with an old woman on it. Aleen leaned close, but he snapped it shut. "You are permitted one last act of large magic." The prophet looked at her. "Before you die."

"One last act," Aleen said. She was thinking, trying to understand.

"Every year on a prophet's birthing day, they can elect to do their one last act of great magic," Bregdon said. "And then they die."

Aleen narrowed her eyes at him. He stared back at her, his eyes glassy in the way that ancient people's are.

"How old are you?" she said.

"Ah," the prophet said. "There is that, too." He grinned a nearly toothless grin. "Prophets live much longer than the ones they love. You will watch them all die. You will be unable to stop it."

Aleen swallowed hard. She did not know if she could do this. If she had a child, if the child had magic, if the child did not choose to become a prophet, would she be able to watch her die?

"So you have not used your last great act," Aleen said, studying the man before her. His skin puckered around his mouth.

"I have never had a reason to use mine," he said. "Yet." He looked at her and tilted his head again. "But I would be willing to pass everything along to you." He paused for a moment. "Everything."

"Why me?" Aleen said.

His eyes widened. "You are needed more than you know, Aleen," he said.

"And why now?" Aleen said.

"I have lost all of those I have loved," Bregdon said. "I have no need of the prophet's Sight anymore. I must pass it to someone else."

"You have no relative who may want it?" Aleen said.

Bregdon shook his head. His white hair, like a halo around his face, shook with it. "No," he said. "Not anymore."

The cottage grew silent.

After many moments, after the old prophet had, in truth, nearly fallen asleep, Aleen spoke again.

"When?" she said.

"My birthday is on the morrow," Bregdon said. "We must meet at midnight. That is when the transfer of powers might begin."

"And this transfer is your last great act of magic?" Aleen said.

Bregdon shook his head. "No," he said.

"What, then?" Aleen said.

Bregdon pointed at her belly. "To give you a child."

She had known. She had known all along that she was barren. She had known it surely, when all these years had passed and she had no child to give her husband. She had known the days she had lost all the others, that hers was not a body that could keep a child.

"Why?" she said. "Why would you sacrifice yourself for me? I am only…" She looked around the cottage. She did not finish her thought.

The prophet smiled. His eyes nearly disappeared in all the folds of skin. Still, Aleen could see the kindness behind it. "I like you, Aleen," he said. He leaned forward. His voice softened. "And I have Seen what you will do."

Aleen narrowed her eyes at Bregdon. "And what if I refuse?" she said. "What of that?"

"You will not," Bregdon said. He leaned back in his chair. "Because the one you love has chosen the way of a prophet as well."

Jem. So Bregdon knew of Jem. Perhaps he knew where Jem was. And if she were a prophet, surely she would be able to find him. Surely she would be able to see him again one day.

And so it was that Aleen accepted the burden that was given her to bear.

Because of Jem. Because of a child. Because hope wears wings in the hearts of its people.

Disappear

The dungeons beneath the dungeons have not grown any warmer in the days since the children have been here. Most of the prophets hang by their very last breaths. They are old, you see. Old and weary. But they hang on for the children. They know they are needed, and sometimes this is all a person needs to hold tightly to life.

The children have developed coughs that worry Aleen. She has heard these coughs before, and they always meant Death. But her birthday is coming, and then, in one great act of magic, she will escape from here. And though the road will not be simple and straight, she has Seen what is next. Her Sight gifted her with that and then quickly faded away forever.

She has Seen what she must do.

So she counts down the hours and waits.

"You will go," Yerin whispers beside her. The children are

sleeping, or at least trying to sleep. They have forgotten day and night, for it is so dark in this dungeon that they do not know how many days and nights pass. "You will go tonight."

"Yes," Aleen says. "On the hour of my birth."

"You will die," he says.

"I am not afraid to die," she says. "For this."

"No," Yerin says. "You were never afraid to die for anything."

Aleen is quiet for a time. She considers. She listens. She lets the voice of yearning open the chambers of her heart, and it does not take long to know whose hand she has been holding all these hours that lead to her birthday. Ah, yes. Yerin. He was not Yerin when she knew him once. He was someone else. But he is one and the same.

He will care for the children like no one else would have cared for them. She knows they will be safe and that she is completely free to do her one last great act. She is permitted to give her life to save them all.

"Jem," she says.

"Yes," he says. "It is I."

"How did you come to be here?" she says.

"In quite the same way you did, my dear," he says. And then: "We have found each other at last."

"And now we must lose each other again," Aleen says.

"But true love endures," he says. "Even after death."

"Yes," she says, for she knows of what he speaks. There are stories that tell of life after death. "I suppose it does."

Yerin wraps his arms around Aleen, and though the dungeon is damp and cold, she feels warm and dry in the circle of him.

"Would that I could go with you," he says.

"You must remain here," she says. "You must take care of the children. They will need you."

"Yes," he says. "I suppose they will."

"They are coming," she says.

"Yes," he says. "I have Seen them, too." And then he pauses. "Did your Sight return?"

Aleen shakes her head. The braids of her hair slither about. "Only momentarily," she says. "Today."

The silence does not feel so thick as it once did, only comforting. Aleen thinks that perhaps he has fallen asleep. So she whispers her next words. "You will not be here forever."

"But you will be gone forever," he says.

"No longer than most," she says. "You will join me. When it is all finished."

Yerin knows this as well. He knows what great act he will be asked to do, one that would commence on the morning of his birthday in six months. And perhaps this, the knowing that they will be together again even in death, is what causes him to chuckle softly, close to her ear. "How fitting," he says, "that we should be together in the end."

"Yes," she says. "How fitting that I should be the one to leave you this time."

"I tried to find you," Yerin says.

"I was practiced at hiding," Aleen says.

"I searched high and low," he says. "And to think, I found you in a dungeon."

"You came here first," Aleen says. His hand strokes hers.

"That I did," Yerin says. "And I shall be here last."

They do not say anything else for some time. They merely lean against one another, Aleen silently counting the hours until she will do her last disappearing act and lift back into the world above the ground and see the stars and the moon and the woman she must find. She knows where the woman is, of course. Her Sight provided that much. She will have perfect aim when the time is right.

For now, she rests. She awaits the hour.

Hazel is staring, as she nearly always is, outside the window that faces her mother's house. She is alone in the house of the

Enchantress. The Enchantress has been gone for some time. A child appears in the distance, then disappears just as quickly. Her mother must have let the children outside for a time. Hazel watches to see if another will appear, but no one does.

And then, as quickly as the child appeared, a whole line of them shows through. Something must have happened to the spell. Hazel rises from her seat. No. They must go back inside. But even the house shaped like a shoe is visible now.

Hazel lifts her staff from where it rests against the entryway wall and moves to the porch of her home. She leans on her staff. The cold traces her cheek. She watches her mother hug the children one by one, as she once hugged Hazel before she came here. She watches Maude kiss their heads and wonders what it is that her mother tells them, where they might possibly be going. The Enchantress has said nothing to her. Has it grown too dangerous for them to stay here? Is that why they have risked moving outside the home that makes them all invisible?

Maude is clearly telling them goodbye. Perhaps she is leaving. Hazel feels a lurch in her chest. Perhaps the children are leaving and Maude is staying. Hazel does not know, cannot know, for the Enchantress…

Where is the Enchantress? Why can Hazel see them all?

And then an ache nearly bends her in two. She would like to tell them goodbye. She would like to see her mother again. If she could let them know how much she loves them and how she will miss them. If she could look in Mercy's eyes again. If she could feel her mother's arms around her.

Something flickers in the corner of her vision. Another movement. Shadows have begun to gather, as if the day is quickly turning to night. It is precisely what is happening, for a wood grows darker more quickly than any open land. The terrors of the forest are beginning to gather as well. At least this is what Hazel first supposes. She sees the children's faces written plainly with fear. Hazel can tell, even from this distance, that Maude is nervous, as if she is unsure whether she should send the children back inside or wait for whatever it is she waits. Perhaps she is meeting someone. Perhaps that someone is not coming.

"Go back inside, Mother," Hazel says, without realizing that she has spoken aloud. "I can see you. Go back inside and take the children. Please."

But Maude, alas, cannot hear the voice of a daughter so far away. She can only watch the world growing dark and wait for the one who does not come.

Again, the flickering in the corner of her vision draws Hazel's eyes toward the wood. Something is moving. Something swift and dark. Something running. Hazel knows, without knowing how, that whatever it is—man or animal or some other danger entirely, has come for the children who wait outside the home that cannot be seen and yet, now, can.

And so it is hope and sadness and desperation and anger that drives Hazel from the house she has been strictly forbidden to leave. It is all of these and more that makes her break free from the enchantment that holds her prisoner. It is all of these and more that makes her raise her staff.

She knows she is supposed to save her magic. She knows she cannot risk using it until it is needed for something important. She knows she could very well die for casting a spell outside the presence of her twin. But there is a man watching. There is a man moving swiftly and relentlessly toward the children. There is a man who will take them. Who is he? She does not know. She only knows that she must be the one who saves them.

Yes, she was supposed to save her magic for something important. But is this not something important? Is this—saving the children and her mother with them—not important enough to risk her very life? She could not save her father or her brother or her best friend, but can she at least do this?

Yes. She can. She will. She will save the children. The Enchantress could do it, but she is not here. She is somewhere else, and there is only Hazel, the running man and Maude and the children. Something must be done.

Hazel begins the incantation. She lifts her staff and points it toward the children. She releases a magic like none the land has ever known, more powerful, even, than the magic of the Enchantress, though she does not know this. And with it, she releases her own power. Hazel crumples to the ground and cannot even open her eyes to see what her spell has done.

Let us see for her, dear reader. Let us see the children who are here one moment and gone the next. Let us see Maude, looking around as though she has lost something and then retreating back into her shoe-shaped house. Let us see the man dressed as a dryad who stops, falls to his knee, rises, clutches his chest, stares, bewildered. Let us watch him turn all about, as if he, too, has lost something.

Where moments ago he saw everything, now he sees nothing. He does not see the girl who lies on the ground outside the invisible home of the Enchantress. He does not see the woman fly inside the door of her shoe-shaped house, where she will sit, alone, and wonder what happened and whether the children are truly safe now. He does not see the children, who have vanished into thin air, each to their separate places, lands far away, where they are, most of all, safe.

He does not, in fact, see anything at all.

The Enchantress, as we speak, is at the castle. She has been held up by the king. First he was not here. And then, when he returned, he merely stared at her. She is well aware of her beauty, of course, but it was quite embarrassing the way he stared, as if her eye held some sway over him.

It is only just now that she has been able to tell him why she has come to the castle. She does not know how late it has grown.

"You know where the children are?" the king says.

"Yes, Your Majesty," she says.

"But I have just hired a Huntsman," the king says.

"You have no need of a Huntsman," the Enchantress says. "I have all the information you desire."

"The Huntsman is already hunting," the king says.

"You need only an Enchantress," she says. "I will take you to them."

"Take the Huntsman, then," the king says.

"He is not here," the Enchantress says.

The king looks around. "Yes, well." He looks back at the Enchantress. "You know where all of them are?"

"All of them," the Enchantress says, but this is not entirely true. She knows where most of them are, but she also knows King Willis is not interested in most. He is only interested in all. But the king will not know her secret for some time. She will find the rest.

"Where are they hiding, did you say?" King Willis says.

"I did not say," the Enchantress says. "They are hiding in the Weeping Woods."

"But the woods burned," King Willis says. "No one survived."

He has said these very words before, if you remember, and was proven wrong, which goes to show that King Willis does not yet fully believe that the children survived.

The Enchantress smiles. "They have magic, Your Majesty," she says. "They can survive much."

"Yes," King Willis says. "I suppose they can. And how is it you know where they live?"

"They live very near me," the Enchantress says. "In a house shaped like a shoe."

Oh, dear. You may have thought you could trust this Enchantress, but it appears that she is giving away an important secret to the very man who was supposed to never know that secret.

"Why have we not found them yet?" the king says.

"It is not so very simple," the Enchantress says. "They live in an invisible house."

"Ah," the king says. He looks on this strange woman with the flashing green eyes. She has a gleam of cruelty buried there, and while it bothers him a bit to be under the spell of a woman, as he supposes he is, he also knows that this partnership might very well be beneficial. She needs him for some reason unknown to him. So he will make his move and she will make her move, and this will be a great game of wits.

"I can uncover it," the Enchantress says. She says nothing about how she is the one who made the home in the first place, or how she struck a deal with the woman who has kept the children safe since the roundup. These things should not be said in the court of a king. So she merely says, "I have the power. They will be in your hands in no time at all."

"And what is it you want from me?" the king says.

"I would like a place in your kingdom," the Enchantress says. "At your right hand."

The king stares at her for a moment. There has never been a woman at the hand of the king. He does not know if he could stand something so foreign and awful. He does not know if he can agree.

And then he remembers his son. "My son," King Willis says. Our king did not realize just how much he had come to enjoy the days when his son stood in the throne room with him. He feels the loss in his chest. Who would have thought that a man like King Willis might feel anything at all for another person? But it is clear, dear reader, that he has begun, against all odds, to love his son. And perhaps it is not only for the future of the kingdom.

"Your son?" the Enchantress says. She pretends to know nothing of what the king says, though, of course, she does.

"My son," the king repeats. "They took him from me."

"The village people," the Enchantress says. "Yes."

"He is alive?" the king says.

"Yes," the Enchantress says. "I have seen him in my looking ball. I have seen him alive, but he is quite changed. You would not recognize him, I fear."

"Changed how?" the king says.

"You shall have to see that for yourself," the Enchantress says with a smile. "He shall be the last child I will deliver to you, after all the others have been found. We will let the people keep him for a time. But certainly not forever."

It is unusual that the king does not argue with the Enchantress. King Willis is a man who wants something and wants it now. Could it be that the Enchantress is truly enchanting? That would surely explain his silence.

"I cannot begin my work until you have agreed to my conditions," the Enchantress says.

"Yes," King Willis says.

"I will have a place in your kingdom?" the Enchantress says, just to be sure. "Your right hand?"

"Granted," the king says, for, at this moment, he has no

other counsel, and, besides, he wants those children once and for all. He wants his son. He wants the kingdom to continue on as it has always done. "Provided you can work with the Huntsman to capture all the children."

"We have no need of a Huntsman," the Enchantress says. "We only have need of me."

"But the Huntsman is an expert at hunting," the king says.

"As am I," the Enchantress says. Her green eyes flutter a little and then widen, as if she knows the hold they have over him.

"I have secured his services already," the king says. "He has a vested interest. A king cannot go back on his word."

The Enchantress can see that she will not win this. She will have to find something to do with that Huntsman. But, for now, she says, "Very well. I will work with your Huntsman. But it is a very simple procedure." She moves closer to the king. He moves back, on impulse, but it is not a quick move, for nothing King Willis does is quick, only sluggishly slow. His lethargy has grown worse in these days after his son's disappearance; he has not eaten and his skin has begun to sag. King Willis, in truth, has begun losing his will. For what good is a kingdom if there is no heir to inherit it?

"Simple," the king says. "Nothing where the children are involved is so simple."

"This is," the Enchantress says. "The children are all in the same place."

The king grins, a slow, wide grin that spreads across his face and makes its way into the hard flint of his eye. "Just so," he says.

Finally, for once, it appears, something is going right for him.

But our king could not be more wrong, as we shall see soon enough.

Future

Aleen and Bregdon met on the eve of the prophet's birthing day. The transfer did not take long. He laid hands on Aleen and spoke words she did not understand, and she felt a great warmth shake into her, and then, at the end of it, a quickening, new life, rising within at the very moment the life of the prophet before her sank into death. His body fell limply to the ground, and she buried him on the top of his hill and went home alone.

Aleen gave birth to a beautiful baby girl, and she was very happy.

She named her daughter Adrian, and she raised her to be good and kind and brave. Adrian had the rare gift of shape-shifting, which Aleen had no knowledge how to tame, but Aleen taught her daughter everything else she knew of magic. Adrian fell in love with a village man Aleen did not like very well, but Aleen knew the ways of love, and she would not keep her daughter from it. She knew that to deny her daughter the beauty of love that she had chosen for herself would be to drive a wedge right down the middle of them all. And so Aleen let Adrian marry the man. And Aleen Saw, in her prophetess way, that her daughter, too, was barren.

But it was a different future she saw for Adrian.

Perhaps it was because Aleen was not ready to die before she could see Jem again, before she could find him, before she could look on his face that was surely wildly different from the one she had once loved. She wanted to meet his family and his children and the people he had come to know in his life. She wanted to assure herself that he had lived a happy life.

And so, rather than give her daughter the gift of a baby, as Bregdon had once given her, Aleen went in search of the baby she had Seen in her visions. She found the child in an abandoned cottage inside some unknown woods, many miles from White Wind.

The baby was fair of skin and quiet of nature, the opposite of Adrian in every way. Aleen picked her up, and the visions she saw shocked her. She knew what this little girl would do. She knew it would not be an easy path for a child. But she knew this girl was the exact right one for what was coming. Aleen would help her. She would see that the girl grew up brave and strong and bold, as she needed to be for the future that would be asked of her.

So she delivered the baby girl to her daughter, and she loved her granddaughter with a love that was vast and wild and fierce enough to keep her visions focused and true all the years of her life, even after her daughter took the child to the land of Fairendale.

The baby girl was called Cora.

Story

It happens in the sharpest instant. A flash. A pop. A single breath. And Yerin is left holding only air. He smiles a bit, though he feels the great sadness spreading inside, for he knows that he has just spent his last chance to hold his beloved. He has just spent his last look on her alive. And now he must begin to do his part.

But he is glad. He is so very glad for what she is doing. She will gift her power to another. Another will carry on her work. The land will be healed. It will take a great many days, of course, but this land will surely be healed.

Yerin falls into a light sleep.

The ground rumbles and shakes, for just a small moment in

time, but it is enough for all the villagers to feel it. They gather, still, inside their secret place. They look around at each other, no one knowing just what the rumbling means but suspecting that it is something important. Something good? Well, that much is left to mystery, for now.

Cora emerges from the room. She moves to the middle of the village, looking off toward the woods. Sir Greyson comes up behind her.

"What is it?" he says.

Cora shakes her head, her eyes clouded. "Something is happening," she says. "Magic."

"But all the magic people are gone," Sir Greyson says.

"So we have been told," Cora says. "But who can really know for sure?" She looks off toward the woods, her eyes straining to see what no eye can see, for no eye has vision enough to look through obstacles like trees that have begun to green again and bushes that widen in the wind and all the debris left from the fire. She cannot see a thing, of course, but sometimes seeing is more than really seeing. Sometimes it is simply a knowing. And Cora can feel in her bones that something is happening, something that will change the course of their stories forever.

"So perhaps there is still magic left in Fairendale?" Sir Greyson says.

"There is always magic in Fairendale," Cora says.

Sir Greyson stares at her, but Cora does not tear her eyes from the woods. "What does it mean?" Sir Greyson says.

"Perhaps it means we shall have more help than we thought," Cora says.

"And perhaps we can win?" Sir Greyson says.

It is only then that Cora turns to him. She smiles at him as if he is nothing more than a child. It is the smile that used to madden him as a young boy, for though she is, in fact, older than him, it is not by much. "We were always going to win," Cora says. "It is what good does."

They watch the woods for what they cannot see.

The Huntsman clutches his chest where the wildest pain he has ever felt spears through him. He is momentarily blinded, unable to see a single bit of what lies before him. His knee hits the ground, and he breathes, in, out, in, out, but it is painful, so very painful. It lasts many moments. But at last it lets him loose, and he rises from the ground, only to find that the children have all vanished.

No. It cannot be.

He looks around the woods. He turns and turns and turns,

but he finds nothing. Nothing. What will he tell the king? He was so very close.

No.

He makes his final turn, back toward the way he has come. It is with great disappointment that he begins to walk.

The Enchantress is on her way back from the castle. She hurries through the woods, for she knows she is hours late for her meeting with Maude and the children, and she is not one for such things as breaking her word. She is almost there when the wood explodes in a blinding wave of light, and an old, bent woman appears in front of her. The woman grabs her arm.

The Enchantress jumps back, but the woman comes with her, will not let her go, clings to her as though she is dying and is desperate for someone to help her live. The Enchantress is powerful, yes, but she cannot bring someone back from death, and it is quite plain to see that this woman is dying.

"I cannot help you," the Enchantress says, trying to shake the old woman off. She is late, after all. She must hurry. There is no time for sympathy.

"It is not you who must help me," the woman says, her voice scratchy. Only her eyes glow in the dark, for her skin is blacker than even the trees. The Enchantress can only see her if she looks away. "It is I who must help you."

"I do not need your help," the Enchantress says. Surely this woman is a vagabond. She appears hungry. The Enchantress can read the hunger in her eyes. "I can give you food," she says. She lifts a pinecone and touches it to her staff. It becomes bread.

The old woman knocks the bread from her hands. Her dark skin is nearly indiscernible in the dark forest. Only her eyes and her teeth show themselves. "I need no bread," the woman says. "I need nothing from you."

"Surely you know you are dying," the Enchantress says.

The old woman grins. Her teeth, in spite of her advanced age, are straight, with not a one missing. The Enchantress tilts her head. "Yes," the old woman says. "I do know this. But before I die…"

"I cannot keep you from dying," the Enchantress says. "Many have tried."

"I do not ask you to keep me from dying," the old woman says. "I do not mind dying so much. For this." She looks around her. The Enchantress thinks that, perhaps, she is talking of the trees and the wood, and she does not understand how a woman would not mind dying for something as barren as the Weeping Woods. What kind of trick is this?

"For what?" the Enchantress says. "For what are you not

afraid to die?"

"For this," the old woman says, and the Enchantress feels a heat begin where the woman's knobby fingers close around her arm. The warmth radiates all the way through the Enchantress. The Enchantress falls to her knees as blackbirds fly around her eyes, round and round and round. When the visions have finished, when the birds have ceased their flying, the old woman lies weak and moaning on the ground.

"What have you done?" the Enchantress says. Her voice is calm, though she feels quite near hysterical now, watching the old woman die. "What have you done to me?"

"I gifted you," the old woman says. "Now use it well." Her head falls back, and a final breath whooshes from her mouth. The Enchantress stands to her feet and looks around, for the first time unsure in which direction she should move.

A snap sounds behind her. She whirls around, but it is too dark to see who might be coming until he is upon her, a tall man with golden-white hair that swings against his shoulders. She cannot see his face, but she hears his grunt. He is as startled to see her as she is to see him.

She knows who he is, of course. She can tell by the concealing clothes he wears. "Huntsman," she says. "What are you doing in the woods this time of night?"

"Collecting," the Huntsman says. "Hunting."

"And did you find that which you hunted?" the Enchantress says. "Did you find the children?"

"Yes," the Huntsman says. "I found them."

The Enchantress looks behind him, but there is no one. "And where are they?" she says.

"I lost them," he says. "They vanished."

The Enchantress glances toward the old woman, but her body is no longer there. "Vanished?" she says.

"Yes," he says. "One minute there, the next gone."

The Enchantress is sure she has misunderstood, for the children did not have magic powerful enough to vanish, unless...

Unless...

She must get back. She must return to her home, but here is this man before her. Might he follow her? She cannot risk it.

"You are returning to the castle now?" she says.

"Yes," the Huntsman says. "I must deliver my news."

"The king will not be happy," the Enchantress says.

"No," the Huntsman says. "He will not."

"Perhaps I should accompany you," the Enchantress says. She turns back toward the way she has just come. "I am in His Majesty's services as well."

"For what?" he says.

"For finding the children," she says. "It appears that we shall work together on this hunt." The Huntsman looks her up and down, as if he does not quite know for sure whether he can trust her. Or perhaps it is because he underestimates a woman of her beauty. Either way, she will show him just what she can do once they have begun their work. She is far more powerful than he is.

"I hope you like sleeping beneath the stars," the Huntsman says. "It appears we shall be hunting after all, though I had hoped it would be simpler."

"Stars," the Enchantress says. "There are no stars anymore."

They both look to the sky.

"Yes, well," the Huntsman says. "Sleeping against the cold earth, then."

"I have my ways," the Enchantress says.

They fall into step, and it is not long before they have cleared the forest and begun their walk along the road to the castle. They do not say anything more until the boy, Garth, opens the castle doors and ushers them into the king's throne room. The king is nearly asleep on his throne. He has not been sleeping well, our poor king, not since his son was stolen from him. He has not been sleeping because he is terrified that the people will come back for him. If his son is taken and if he is stolen, what hope is there for saving the kingdom? None.

King Willis looks up upon their arrival.

"Ah," he says. "I did not expect you to return so soon."

"We come with news, Your Majesty," the Enchantress says.

"Yes," the king says. "Very well." He smiles, for he has been awaiting news but did not dare hope that it would come in the very same day he met these two. How fortunate.

The Enchantress glances at the Huntsman. His eyes watch her. She has seen those wild blue eyes somewhere. Does she know this man? Have they only just met or are there years that stretch between them? She looks away before she can answer that question.

"Enchantress," the king says. "Tell me, what news do you bring?"

The Enchantress gestures toward the Huntsman and says, "He shall tell you, Your Majesty."

The blue eyes grow dark now, as if they have shifted from a morning sky to evening. The Huntsman turns his gaze upon the king. It is sometimes easier to say what must be said quickly. So he says, "I have lost the children."

"We have lost the children," the Enchantress says.

"Lost the children?" the king says. He appears confused, as if he does not understand quite how this might have happened, yet again. "How have you lost the children? You said they were all in one place."

"They vanished," the Huntsman says. "Before my very eyes."

"But no matter," the Enchantress says. "We shall find them

again. They cannot hide from my looking ball."

"Disappeared? Before your very eyes?" the king says. "How can this be?"

"Powerful magic," the Enchantress says. "Though not nearly as powerful as mine."

"Your magic," the king says. "How do we know it was not your magic that made the children disappear?" King Willis squints his eyes. The Enchantress tilts her head.

"Why, I was at the castle, sire," the Enchantress says. "You had only just told me to gather the children."

"It is true, sire," the Huntsman says, extending his hand to the tall woman beside him. He is taller than she, but not by much. "This woman was not anywhere near the children.

The king roars. The Enchantress, though, does not even blink. She is not afraid of an angry king. She and the Huntsman wait for the king's next move. He looks at both of them, from one to the other. "So, tell me," he says. "What is it we shall do?"

"I know a way to find the children," the Enchantress says. "All of them." She smiles at her king, dazzling him in the glow. He feels the corners of his lips pull up as well, though he did not intend to smile. It is not the kind of circumstances that deserve a smile. These two have just lost the children, once again, when they were at the king's fingertips.

"How?" King Willis says.

"It will take time," the Enchantress says. "I suspect they have separated." She glances at the Huntsman, who is looking at her. "To make our hunt more difficult."

"How long?" the king says.

"Months, perhaps," the Enchantress says. "Will you be able to wait for months?"

The king roars again, and the sound of it bounces against the marble floor and up to the ornate ceiling and around on the white walls. "How will you find them?" the king says, when he has again calmed himself.

"We will hunt them down, one by one," the Enchantress says. The Huntsman nods, though no one is looking at him.

"Every one of them?" the king says.

"Every one of them," the Enchantress says. The king looks at her, and after a space of three breaths, he nods his head.

"Very well," he says. "You will have another chance. Show me you can do this, and you will have a place in my kingdom."

The Enchantress dips her head.

"And you," the king says, pointing at the Huntsman, "will go with her, to collect the children and bring them to me."

"I have a plan for that as well," the Enchantress says.

"Perhaps you do," the Huntsman says. "But I will accompany you."

"Yes, he will," the king says. He narrows his eyes at the

Enchantress. "Perhaps I cannot trust you alone, but together?" He seems to consider this question for a moment. "Yes, perhaps together."

All is quiet in the hall as the Huntsman and the Enchantress wait to be dismissed. But the king has another question. "How will you find them?" King Willis says. "When no one else could?"

The Enchantress smiles once more, but her lips do not reveal her white teeth this time. "I have a looking ball," she says.

The king is silent. He has only heard of looking balls in stories. "And how will your looking ball find them?" he says, for he has always wanted to understand this magic.

"Because I touched them," the Enchantress says.

This bit of information may seem strange to you, dear reader. But this is yet another of the mysterious rules of magic that Arthur so diligently taught the magical children during their magic lessons in the village, though none of them knew about the magic ball so close to their shoe-shaped home, for they had never seen it, and, in truth, never listened to a single word Arthur said when it did not seem to apply to them. What need did they have of the rules of magic looking balls? So even if they had known about the magic ball, they would not have known its significance. If, perhaps, Hazel could have seen her mother or any of the children after entering the house of the Enchantress, she might have warned them of this danger. The owner of a magic looking ball, you see, has only to touch a person to connect that person's body to the ball, meaning that the owner will be able to see everything about that person—where she goes, what he does, how they might transform to remain hidden. On her last visit to Maude's house, the Enchantress touched the head of every child before she left. Her ball holds them all.

"You have touched them?" the king says, for not many know about the rules of a looking ball.

"Yes," the Enchantress says. "It is all I need to see them in my ball."

"Brilliant," the king says, and his voice holds all the excitement it can possibly contain. The children will surely be found this time, with the help of a ball that can see them all. "Absolutely brilliant." He says the words over and over and over again, until the Enchantress and the Huntsman look at one another and wonder if, perhaps, they should leave of their own accord, for the king does not seem as well as he did when they first appeared in the throne room.

This is what one might call shock, dear reader. Sometimes an awful thing does not catch up to a person until many hours or days or even weeks later. The shock of losing a son, of losing the entire king's guard, of failing in what seemed like a simple plan, can turn a man's heart fragile and his mind a bit toward madness. Our poor king has had quite a few shocks already.

And there is another one coming. The king does not even know about this one.

Let us watch King Willis for a moment. Let us look on his squinty eyes and listen to his raucous laugh and the words that continue to stream from his mouth, "Brilliant. Absolutely brilliant. Brilliant." Let us think of all he has been through. He, a man who desires to keep his throne at all costs, has lost his son and his king's guard, and he has failed to secure his throne. This is the kind of pressure that can make a man break once and for all. King Willis, dear reader, is breaking. But sometimes what has been broken can also be restored so it is much greater and truer than it was before. This, of course, is always the hope that comes with breaking. We may hope for him. We may hope that in his breaking, King Willis will be put back together in a better, kinder, truer way.

The Enchantress speaks into the enormous void that is left when the king's laughter has died out into tears. "The children shall be found. Do not worry, my king."

She touches the Huntsman on his shoulder. He turns with her, and both of them leave the king's presence.

At the doors of the castle, the Huntsman turns to the Enchantress. "Shall we begin straight away?" he says.

"Yes," says the Enchantress. "Let us begin."

Back in the throne room, the king hunches on his throne. The tears still fall, and there is nothing he can do to stop them. Does he grieve for his men? Does he grieve for his son? Does he grieve for a kingdom that cannot be secured until all the missing children have been found?

It is all of these. It is everything. It is…

Well, perhaps we should leave our king to his grief.

But wait. The curtain covering the long, slender mirror that stands fifteen feet from the throne billows and then, without even a hand touching it, pillows to the floor. King Willis looks up at its whisper of sound. He sees the mirror. He rises. He moves toward it.

The mirror will surely tell him what is next, as it has always done.

He stops when his reflection touches every border of the mirror. He is not as close to it as some might be if they wanted their form to touch every side, for he is, after all, a large man. He reaches out his hand, but he is too far away to touch the golden flourishes that line the mirror. He stares at his reflection, waiting for it to speak. This is how it has always happened.

But this time something is different. This time the form

inside the mirror shakes and shifts. This time it becomes the form of his father.

And then his father speaks. King Willis stumbles back, tripping over his own feet and then a stair and then the leg of the throne, which has just—has it moved its golden leg? Could that even be possible? Could a throne come alive and trip a king?

King Willis falls to the ground with a heavy thud, and the world grows dark around him.

Surely not. Surely that was not his father. Surely he is going mad.

These thoughts join a host of troubled dreams. Our king sleeps. But do not worry, dear reader. It is not forever. There is still much King Willis will do in our story.

For now, we will leave him, crumpled up on the floor, where it will take hours for one of his servants to find him.

Deep in the dungeons beneath the dungeons the children have just woken in their places around the cell. They feel the absence of the prophetess like a cold blanket has descended upon this home where they have spent far too many days. Aleen, you see, brought a warmth and a comfort inside the bars. And now she is gone.

"Where is Aleen?" says one of the children.

"She is gone," Yerin says. His voice breaks on his words.

"Why did she leave us?" another child says. "Why did she not take us with her?"

"She could not take us with her," Yerin says. "She did not have that much magic left."

"But why did she go?" the same child says.

"She had to do what she could while she could," Yerin says. He pats the child, who has moved closer to him in the dark, on his rigid back. He is just a young thing. Small and curled up on the cold floor. Yerin pulls the boy into his arms, in a way he never did for his boy. He regrets it like nothing else. Perhaps if he had embraced his boy more often, he might have become someone entirely different.

"She had magic left?" the child says. "Why did she not leave much sooner?"

"Because the only magic a prophet has is summoned on the prophet's birthing day," Yerin says.

"Today is her birthing day?" the child says.

"Yes," Yerin says. "It is."

"I wish I could tell her happy birthing day," the child says.

"Yes, well," Yerin says.

"I wish I could tell her I love her," a girl calls out in the dark, from somewhere behind Yerin.

"I am sure she knew it already," Yerin says.

"What is she doing to help save us?" says the child in Yerin's lap.

Yerin squeezes the child again. What he would do to embrace his son again. But it is too late for that. His son died long ago. "That we cannot know," Yerin says. "But what we can know is this: the wheels have been set in motion. And no one can stop them."

"Not even the evil King Willis?" the boy says.

"The king is not so very evil," Yerin says, though he does not expect the children to understand. But perhaps a story. Stories can teach them what they do not yet know. So Yerin says, "Would you like to hear a story?"

The boy in his lap answers for all the other children. "Yes, very much," he says.

"Gather round, children," Yerin says. He waits for the dungeon to grow quiet again before he begins. He weaves around them a magnificent story of impossible escape and valiant rescue and happily ever after.

Will this one be a magnificent story of impossible escape and valiant rescue and happily ever after?

Well, now, we shall have to wait and see.

Don't miss out on the next Fairendale adventure!

What's the real story behind how Rumpelstiltskin became Rumpelstiltskin? Find out in Book 7: *The Boy Who Spun Gold*.

The Delicate Art of Prophecy

By Aleen
Prophetess of White Wind

Prophecy is a strange sort of gift. It is bestowed in unequal measure—some contain within them a greater gift of prophecy than others. Some can see whole years beyond the current moment, while some can only see a day or two beyond. Some see in clear pictures. Some see with a haze over the picture.

Some of the minor prophets in the land can only see something a moment before it happens and can only hope that their course of action or interference will do some good in the world.

It is not guaranteed that all who choose to become prophets will become prophets. Only those with the most powerful gifts of magic are given the gift of prophecy, and even powerful magic is not guarantee. Prophecy, you see, is quite powerful and has a mind of its own.

It is not a gift that can be easily carried but must be weighed and used for the good of the land as a whole. Not all people need to know the future, but when some do, it is the prophets' responsibility to tell them. This is not always easy, but it is required of a prophet. So a prophet, more than anything else, must be judicious and discerning.

With shifting visions, difficult decisions, and the weight that can come from knowing something that others do not know, there is a delicate art to mastering prophecy.

Here are my best tips:

1. Do not force it.

There is not a gift on earth that can be forced into being. Some are simply not given the gift, even after they choose to become a prophet. It is not worthwhile to force yourself to see the future. Some parents believe that their children must have this gift and so will painstakingly prepare them for it right along with their regular education. At least, this is how prophecy worked in the old days, before magic became something suspicious in the minds of the people.

A gift of prophecy can never be forced. It can only be channeled.

2. Use your gift always for good.

This is one of the sacred rules surrounding prophecy, but it is not always clear what "good" means. Good means different things to different people. For example, is it good to use your gift of prophecy to save someone you love? Is it good to use your gift of prophecy to further the advance of dark magic if you have Seen the light win in the end? Is it good to use your gift of prophecy to gift another sorceress with your entire store of dark magic so that she might save the realm—or not?

The shifting winds of good must be weighed carefully in the mind and heart of every prophet.

3. Be as unaffected by what you have seen as you possibly can be.

I admit that this can be one of the most difficult parts of being a prophet. Sometimes a prophet will see death and destruction, and it is difficult not to give in to fear and weeping and the nearly uncontrollable urge to change it all for the better. Sometimes what you see is so wonderful that you cannot help but tell those to whom good things are coming, but this is not always best, either. How significantly is joy diminished by knowing that something is coming before it comes?

4. Do not worry about what other people think.

As a prophet, you will be called many untrue things. You will be called mad, which is the gentlest of the people's bellicose names. You will also be called traitor, liar, dark sorcerer, and you must not let any of these sway your decision to share your Vision. A prophet must be brave at all costs.

Not only this, but prophets have some strange tendencies. For example, when receiving a Vision, a prophet's eyes will glaze over and appear completely empty, as though no one is home. Sometimes a prophet is shaken physically by a Vision, and limbs will do whatever limbs will do. Sometimes a prophet will be unable to control what comes from her mouth, often chanting for hours on end. Do not concern yourself with what others think of you. You are called to something greater.

Prophecy, as you can see, is not for the faint of heart. It is a gift that must be received and held with great care.

And if you should find yourself a prophet, welcome to the fold.

The Sacred Rules of Prophets

By the Founding Council of Prophets
All the lands

You must only use your prophesying gift for good.

You must not use your gift for your own gain. Ever.

You must tell the future exactly as you have seen it unfold before you.

You must decide whether you would like to become a prophet before your first child is born, trading your gift of magic for a gift of prophecy.

If you decide to become a prophet, you cannot ever have your magic gift restored by the Old Man's Great Book, which is sometimes a possibility. The possibility of restoring a magical gift remains if one does not choose to become a prophet and simply lets the magic fade away upon bearing a child.

Upon becoming a prophet, you are only permitted to use your former gift of magic one more time, on one of your birthing days. After you use this last bit of magic, you die.

Those who choose to become prophets retain limited immortality. (What is limited immortality? It is this: If you use your gift of prophecy well, you live. If you do not, you die. It is anyone's guess what "well" means.)

Necessary Tools of the Prophets

By Yerin
Prophet of Lincastle

A magical staff: Prophets do not need a staff for prophesying, but they can be useful as the years move on and a back becomes bent. Most prophets use their magical staffs while they walk. Sometimes the staffs assist them in their Visions, though no one knows how much connection remains between a prophet and his former magical staff. Those who are no longer in possession of their staffs tend to lose their ability to prophesy.

A third eye: The third eye is what allows a prophet to see into the future. It is bestowed upon a prophet when he or she agrees to trade the gift of magic for the gift of prophecy.

A knowledge of the Old Man's Great Book: The Old Man's Great Book is an enchanted book that contains all the spells possible in the land of Fairendale and those beyond, including the spell that can restore the magical powers of those worthy of restoration. Every prophet must have at least a working knowledge of this book, usually obtained while they practiced their magic in former years. The Old Man's Great Book is the foundation of any proper magical training.

The Old Man's Great Book contains vital information about prophecy as well, but, unfortunately, there are only three in existence—one with the Evil Queen, whom you will meet in

Book 7; one inside the library of Fairendale castle, taken off the person of Aleen, prophetess of White Wind, when she was imprisoned in the dungeons beneath the dungeons; and one that has mysteriously disappeared.

The Old Man's Great Book was written and compiled by the prophet Bregdon of White Wind, who is otherwise known as the Old Man.

The Royal Family of Fairendale

King Willis: The current king of Fairendale. Has a deep love for sweet rolls, and it shows in his, well, wideness.

Queen Clarion: The current queen of Fairendale. Is underestimated by her husband, but we shall see just how powerful she is soon enough.

Prince Virgil: Son of King Willis and Queen Clarion, best friend of Theo. Prefers rye bread with melted butter to sweet rolls, depending on the day.

King Sebastien: Deceased king of Fairendale, exception to the line of boys who tried to steal thrones and were, upon failing at their quest, forever banished to sail the Violet Sea. Was killed by a blackbird.

The Villagers of Fairendale

Arthur: Village furniture maker and magic instructor to girls who possess the gift of magic. Is a bit reckless but always manages to come out on the other side—though one is not always assured it will be so.

Maude: Arthur's wife. Bakes spectacular pumpkin sugar cookies. Prefers caution to reckless abandon.

Hazel: Daughter of Arthur and Maude, twin of Theo. Cares for the village sheep and can even, amazingly, understand them.

Theo: Son of Arthur and Maude, twin of Hazel. Finishes his chores early so he can sit in on magic lessons.

Mercy: Daughter of Cora, best friend of Hazel. Prefers spectacular acts of magic to "boring" ones.

Cora: Mother of Mercy, widow, shape shifter. A woman who moves.

Garron: The town gardener. Talks to plants as though they can hear him. Has three sons: 12-year-old twins and a 13-year-old.

Bertie: The town baker. Enjoys showing off his air-kneading skills for the children.

Staff of Fairendale Castle

Garth: Page for King Willis, the oldest of twelve children. Sometimes calls King Willis "Your Wideness."

Cook: One of the few shape shifters in the land. Shape shifts into a bear. Is highly annoyed by her assistant, Calvin.

Calvin: An orphan who began working as Cook's assistant instead of traveling to live with distant relatives in Ashvale—and so did not perish in the Fire Mountain that claimed the entire population of Ashvale many years ago. Tasked with feeding the prisoners in the dungeons beneath the dungeons.

Sir Greyson: Captain of the king's guard. Receives medicine, which keeps his mother alive, in exchange for his service to the king. Carries a magical sword that cannot be lifted by any but him.

Sir Merrick: Second in command to Sir Greyson.

Important Prophets

Aleen: A prophetess who is one hundred forty-two years old, from the kingdom of White Wind. Wears ebony skin and what appears to be a collection of snakes for hair (though it is not).

Yerin: A prophet who is one hundred forty-two years old, from the wild woodland between Lincastle and Eastermoor. Has white hair that makes the dark of the dungeons where he is imprisoned a bit less dark.

Dragons of Morad

Zorag: King of the dragons of Morad. Lost his parents in the Great Battle, when King Sebastien stole the throne from the Good King Brendon. Would like nothing more than peace.

Blindell: Zorag's cousin, raised as the dragon king's son. Lost his parents in the Great Battle, when King Sebastien stole the throne from the Good King Brendon. Would like nothing more than revenge.

Larus: One of the elder dragons of Morad, male. Counselor to Zorag.

Malera: One of the elder dragons of Morad, female.

Counselor to Zorag.

The lost 12-year-old children of Fairendale

Ursula

Chester

Charles

Thumbelina (known as Lina among the children)

Minnie

Jasper

Frederick

Ruby

Martin

Oscar

Homer

Anna

Aurora

Rose

Edgar

Harriet (known as Hattie among the children)

Isabel (known as Izzy among the children)

Ralph

Dorothy

Julian

Tom Thumb

Philip

About the Author

While she has never possessed the gift of magic, L.R.'s teachers claimed she had a gift for words, which one might agree is quite like a gift of magic. Bringing a story to life that did not exist before is very much like transforming an old shoe into a dish towel. L.R. feels quite honored that she was given this gift and hopes to use it to encourage other young writers to discover their own gifts, for what is the world without words and stories?

L.R. is the queen of her castle in San Antonio, TX. She lives with her king and her six young princes, who daily give her inspiration for more grand tales of magic and adventure.

www.lrpatton.com

A Note From L.R.

I hope you've enjoyed reading this book from the annals of Fairendale's history. The world of Fairendale has been a lovely world to create, and I've had fun sketching maps, re-reading fairy tales and thinking, endlessly, about characters and their plights—because a series like this one takes lots and lots of time and hard work. But because it's always been my dream to create a fantasy world and share it with my readers, I knew it was something I had to do. (So, you see, dreams really do come true.)

If you have any questions about Fairendale or simply want to send me a note to tell me who your favorite character is or what kinds of extras you'd like to see me release in the future (a *Creatures of the Violet Sea* is coming soon!), email me at lr@lrpatton.com. I always enjoy hearing from my young readers.

Please consider leaving (or ask your parent to leave) a review of this book wherever you bought it. Reviews help get books into the hands of potential new readers, which is incredibly important for authors like me. And don't forget to pick up your free bonus materials when you stop by my web site! (www.lrpatton.com)

Thank you so much for supporting my work.

In love,

L.R.

Enjoy more stories from the magical Fairendale series:

LRPatton.com/Fairendale